To:
THE Hendrick
Family

Thanks for your friendship
These many years!
Enjoy the fantastical
journey into
NELINIA!

Ryann Watters
and the
King's Sword
Eric Reinhold

BOOK 1
The Annals of Aeliana

CREATION
HOUSE
A STRANG COMPANY

RYANN WATTERS AND THE KING'S SWORD by Eric Reinhold
Published by Creation House
A Strang Company
600 Rinehart Road
Lake Mary, Florida 32746
www.creationhouse.com

Scripture quotations are from the Holy Bible, New International Version. Copyright © 1973, 1978, 1984, International Bible Society. Used by permission; also the King James Version of the Bible; and the New American Standard Bible. Copyright © 1960, 1962, 1963, 1968, 1971, 1972, 1973, 1975, 1977 by the Lockman Foundation. Used by permission. (www.Lockman.org)

Cover design by Amanda Potter

Cover art and illustrations by Corey Wolfe, www.coreywolfe.com

Library of Congress Control Number: 2007938626
International Standard Book Number: 978-1-59979-288-0

First Edition

08 09 10 11 12 — 9 8 7 6 5 4 3 2 1
Printed in the United States of America

For Kaylyn,
Kara, and Kyler,
who stimulated
my imagination with
nightly requests for
impromptu fantasy tales.

Acknowledgments

OVER A SEVEN-YEAR period, from beginning this effort to its conclusion, there are many people to thank. First and foremost, I need to start at the beginning with my three children: Kaylyn, Kara, and Kyler. Every night they would encourage me at bedtime to continue telling the ongoing story of three kids and their fantastic exploits. Most evenings it was on the fly, and other days I would find myself pondering ahead of time what new circumstances I could engage the characters in. They always said I should make these stories into a book so that other kids could enjoy them.

To my wife, Kim: I cannot express enough gratitude for your unselfish homeschooling of our children and unconditional love for me. I am the dreamer and you are the realist. Thanks for providing an environment for me to fulfill one of my dreams!

To my parents: you laid the Christian foundation in my life and encouraged me in everything I pursued. Thank you for fostering the desire to travel and experience new things; it was key in developing my imagination. I love you both.

To my brother Baron: we forged a bond of experiences at the Naval Academy that continue to grow grander and more outlandish each year. I acknowledge that you had "the last real plebe year," only because my class trained you!

My brother Johnny: despite my leaving for college when you were only five, I'm thankful that we've been able to develop a close relationship as you entered adulthood.

My sister, Kerstin: your early blondhood, world exploits, degrees, and culmination into counselor and mother have provided me with much laughter and respect.

I love the three of you, my dear siblings.

To Lois Blackburn, family friend and my first editor: thank you for taking untold hours to read my original work and spill enough red ink to create a crime scene. You can take credit for getting me in shape as a writer.

To seven lifelong friends, Matt Balters, Simon Bailey, Alfred Bunge, Dan Pugh, Keith Hendrick, Shane Smith, and Arto Woodley, who will take a phone call from me at any hour on any continent, sincerely listen, provide honest feedback and prayer: you guys are the best. One true friend is a treasure, and I've found more than my fair share.

To Greg Hauenstein, my youth pastor at Old Cutler Presbyterian Church in Miami: you had a huge impact on my spiritual development. To Westminster Christian School: I thank you for watering the seeds of talent God gave me in academics and athletics, but most importantly for conveying God's Word through a wonderful staff of teachers.

Thank you to the United States Naval Academy for helping develop the character traits of integrity, accountability, discipline, perseverance, leadership, commitment, and patriotism. The Naval Academy Preparatory School, four years in Annapolis, and six as a naval officer left an indelible stamp on my life and can be seen on my business Web site at www.academy wealth.com.

To Pat Morley for helping me discern between being religious and being a Christian. Thanks to the Greater Orlando Leadership Foundation (now Lifework Leadership) for exposing me to a network of believers in the Orlando business community and stimulating my faith.

To three mentors in my primary business of financial planning, Charlie Woodward, Paul Kraus, and Harry Horn: all three of you played a progressing role in my business development. Thanks to Chad Watson for being a conduit from the Navy to my civilian career, to Austin Pryor for your sound counsel, and Ron Blue for your spiritual insights with Kingdom Advisors.

Thank you to First Baptist Sweetwater, my church family since 1994. You've provided a wonderful foundation for my children to grow up in. Special thanks to the Cross Trainers for putting up with my teaching (http://crosstrainers-fbs.blogspot .com). I've secretly always wanted to have my book adorn the walls of our library. I hope this is the first of many.

Special thanks to more recent people who have come into my life: JoAnn, my right arm at work, for balancing my schedule and making everything work for my clients; to Ezies Ebrahim for praying for me; to Jane Frank, who provided insightful commentary on my work as I put on the finishing touches; to Mrs. Warner's ninth grade honors English classes for reviewing the rough draft and providing honest feedback; and to Abigail Pugh for the most insightful student feedback an author could ask for.

I would also like to thank Corey Wolfe, the artist who responded to my e-mail, took a step of faith, and embraced my project. He captured my thoughts and expressions to lay out a book cover that, in my humble opinion, is second to none in the youth fiction genre. Thanks, Corey; I hope our mutual passion translates to eager and excited readers for many years to come.

Lastly, I would like to thank Steve Strang for opening the door of opportunity at Creation House, and for their team enlisting the editorial skills of Larry Leech to hone my tale into a more enjoyable read. Your insights were most welcome and helpful.

Beyond the human thanks, I must thank God for the time, treasure, and talent He has graciously chosen to give me. I pray that my efforts would be worthy of a fatherly grin to His beloved child.

Contents

Foreword

To the Town of Mount Dora

Seven years ago, when I began the research phase of writing my book, I knew I needed a unique town. Key requirements were a lake, interesting alleyways, fanciful shops, and other dynamic features that would engage the reader. My first inclination was to create a fictitious town in the mountains of North Carolina, which would give me the freedom to create whatever my heart desired. A few weeks later I ventured twenty miles west of my home and rediscovered Mount Dora. Over the course of the day, between walking the streets and driving around, I found every element an author could desire to create a fantastical adventure.

During the first year, I quickly outlined the book and wrote eleven chapters. It was my intent to be published in 2001, certainly no later than 2002. Alas, life is like a mountain highway on a moonless night, and even with high beams we can only see a few hundred feet in front of us. Between the events of September 11, 2001, personal health issues, getting my "real" business off the ground, raising my children, and trying to be a loving husband, my project was shelved. Periodically I would stumble across my marked-up manuscript pouting back at me, neglected.

At the midpoint of 2007 I heard the cry. Maybe it was due to the issues above coming to a point where there wasn't so much noise in the foreground. More probable was the fact that God had brought me to a place where I was listening again. The cry didn't come out audibly as "finish me... finish me," but there was a sense that if I didn't nurture the project back to life it would decompose into a good intention. Anyone who knows me also knows that I am not one to start something and not finish it. I hope that it is an issue of perseverance and not pride. I believe everything happens for a purpose and in the appropriate timing, and the completion of this novel is no exception. Many of the people I mention in my acknowledgments are people who came into my life between 2001 and 2007.

I had been back to Mount Dora many times since 2002; however, I wasn't quite prepared for the myriad of changes that occurred over the past few years. My desire to use a real town was so readers could more easily relate to my story and see themselves in it. Technology has advanced so much during that period that digital photography is commonplace and everyone uses a computer and the Internet—certainly my readers. What better way to capture the realism of a book than to point to a Web site which provides the photography of the actual setting and detailed artwork of the characters. It is my dream the Ryann Watters series rides the crest of the wave of the new interactive media and "old fashioned" print at www.RyannWatters.com.

Some of the changes that took place over those six to seven years were spectacular for the city of Mount Dora, and others are part of the sorrow of progress. Among the improvements, Mount Dora completely updated their senior high and middle schools. The middle school I describe in the first few chapters no longer exists; however, I kept it anyway because the dilapidated structures fit so well with the storyline. Even with progress, Mount Dora is cleaner than it has ever been, and I would bet there are more American flags per square foot than any town in America! In addition, I was surprised upon my return to see the additions the First Presbyterian Church of Mount Dora had added. The backside of the church changed from the old alleyway look with the park bench that Noah would sleep on, but again, I saw no need to change the storyline. The one grave issue with progress, especially in a growing town, is that the old-timers tend to get squeezed out. In this case, one of my favorite bookstores anywhere met its demise. Dickens-Reed Bookstore was the best—from the carved-book façade out front, which still remains (I had my picture taken in front of it for this book), to the checker/chess tables, coffee bar, and fantastical children's section; this store topped the charts. I had to keep it, but went ahead and had Ryann allude to the fact that it might be meeting an early demise.

So, to Mount Dora I say, "Thank you!" Thanks for the setting, the patriotism, the cleanliness, the lake, railroad, stores, alleyways, lighthouse, tradition, and so much more. My hope is that this book and series only enhances your charm and that those who read it will have a desire well up in their heart to visit and experience you for themselves.

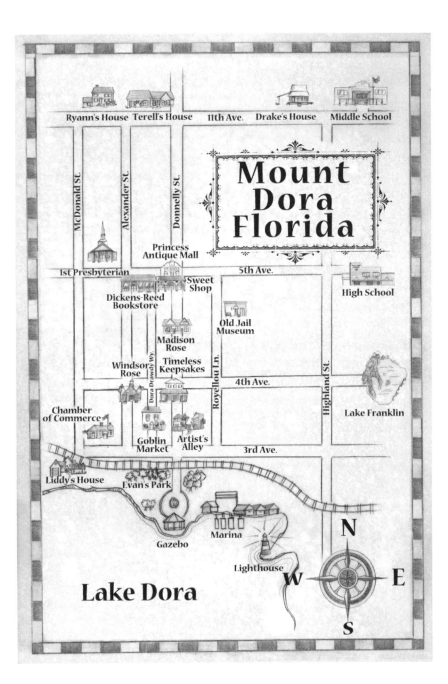

Mount
Dora
Florida

Ryann's House Terell's House 11th Ave. Drake's House Middle School

McDonald St.

Alexander St.

Donnelly St.

Princess
Antique Mall

1st Presbyterian   5th Ave.   High School

Sweet
Shop

Dickens-Reed
Bookstore

Old Jail
Museum

Madison
Rose

Dora Drawdy Wy.

Windsor Timeless
Rose   Keepsakes

Royellou Ln.

Highland St.

4th Ave.

Lake Franklin

Chamber
of Commerce

Goblin   Artist's
Market   Alley

3rd Ave.

Liddy's House

Evan's Park

Gazebo

Marina

Lighthouse

N
W   E
S

Lake Dora

4

AELIANA

Joynnted Knolls

Tree of Life

Myraddin

Dryn River

Glenys Falls

Elan River

Boulders

Lake Penwyn

Peda River

Canyon

Marrow Mountains

Western Forrest

N
W   E
S

Morganwy Sea

Ryann Watters

Without a watch, Ryann would be lost. In one sense he is carefree and loves to joke around, yet he is also very aware of what time of day it is and whether the events of the day are on schedule. Classmates like him and he's a natural leader. A strength that can be a weakness is his competitive nature and always wanting to be first at everything.

> **LITTLE KNOWN FACT:**
>
> *Ryann enjoys watching sports and is thinking about trying out for the basketball team.*

Terell Peterson

Ryann's best friend, Terell, moved into his neighborhood two years ago from the big city streets of Atlanta. His mother teaches at the high school. Terell enjoys fishing around the numerous lakes in Mount Dora and biking along the picturesque streets. He is self-conscious about his stuttering, and his deepest desire is to overcome his timidity and be stronger.

LITTLE KNOWN FACT:

Terell wants to be an artist someday and dreams about finding someone with whom he can apprentice.

Liddy Thomas

When you look up *smart*, *athletic*, and *pretty* in the dictionary, Liddy's name pops up. She seems to have it all together, but sometimes her desire to have everything scientifically proven can be her greatest weakness. Not easily intimidated, this talented soccer player with an expansive vocabulary has developed a close friendship with Ryann and Terell.

LITTLE KNOWN FACT:

Liddy secretly enjoys sewing but feels others might make fun of her hobby.

Drake Dunfellow

Drake is the opposite of Liddy—everything in life seems to be going against him. Living with his eerie aunt and backwards uncle after his parents died prematurely in a car accident, Drake has allowed bitterness to take root in his heart. Held back a year in school due to this hardship, Drake isolates himself and lashes out in anger at classmates.

> **LITTLE KNOWN FACT:**
>
> *Drake loves the thrill of roller coasters. His three favorites in nearby Orlando are Universal's Hulk, Sea World's Kraken, and Disney World Animal Kingdom's Expedition Everest.*

Discover the Powers and Record Them Here

Ring:

- White- _____
- Black- _____
- Red- _____
- Green- _____
- Blue- _____
- Yellow- _____
- Orange- _____
- Gold- _____

Staff:

- Button 1- _____
- Button 2- _____
- Button 3- _____
- Button 4- _____
- Button 5- _____
- Button 6- _____
- Button 7- _____

Horn:

- 1 Long Blast- _____
- 3 Short Blasts- _____
- 7 Short Blasts- _____

CHAPTER 1

The
Angel's Visitation

T FIRST APPEARED as a gentle glow, almost like a child's night-light. Heavy shadows filled the room as the boy lay face up, covers tucked neatly under his arms. A slight smile on his face hinted that he was in the midst of a pleasant dream.

Ryann Watters, who had just celebrated his twelfth birthday, rolled lazily onto his side, his blond hair matted into the pillow, unaware of the glow as it began to intensify. Shadows searched for hiding places throughout the room as the glow transformed from a pale yellow hue to brilliant white.

Ryann's eyelids fluttered briefly and then flickered at the glare reflecting off his pale blue bedroom walls. Drowsily, he turned toward the light expecting to see one of his parents coming in to check on him. "What's going on?" his voice cracked as he reached up to rub the crusty sleep from his eyes.

Under a pale half-moon, Drake Dunfellow's house looked just like any other. A closer inspection, however, would reveal its failing condition. Water oaks lining the side of the curved driveway hunched over haggardly, like old men struggling on canes. The lawn, which should have been a lively green for early spring, was withered and sandy. A few patches of grass were sprinkled here and there. Rust lines streaked down the one jagged peak atop the tin-roof house. The flimsy clapboard sides were outlined by fading white trim speckled with dried paint curls. Hanging baskets containing a variety of plants and weeds all struggling to stay alive shared the crowded front porch with two mildew-covered rocking chairs. Inside, magazines and newspaper clippings both old and new were carelessly strewn about. Encrusted dishes from the previous day's meals battled each other for space in the bulging kitchen sink. In the garage, away from the usual living areas, was a boy's room. Dull paneling outlined the bedroom, while equally dreary brown linoleum covered the floor. The bedroom must have been an afterthought because not much consideration had been given to the details. A bookcase cut from rough planks sat atop an old garage sale dresser.

Moonlight pressing through the dust-covered metal blinds tried to provide a sense of peacefulness. Instead it revealed bristly red hair atop a young boy's head poking out from beneath a mushy feather pillow. His heavy breathing provided the only movement in the quiet room. Tiny droplets of perspiration lined his brow as he began jerking about under the thin cotton sheets.

Starting at the edge of the window, the blackness spread downward, transforming all traces of light to an oily dinginess. Drake was slowly surrounded and remained the only thing not saturated in the darkness. Bolting upright to a stiff-seated attention, Drake's bloodshot eyes darted back and forth. He stared into the black nothingness shuddering and aware that the only thing visible in the room was his bed.

"Who…who's there?" Drake cried out, puzzled by the hollow sound that didn't seem to travel beyond the edge of his mattress. Beads of sweat trickled down his neck, connecting his numerous freckled dots. He strained, slightly tilting his head, ears perked. There was no reply.

Neatly manicured streets wandered through the Watters's sleepy, rolling neighborhood. If someone had been walking along in the wee morning hours of March 15, they would have noticed the brilliant white light peeking out from around Ryann's shade. Below his second-story window the normally darkened bed of pink, red, and white impatiens was lit up as in the noonday sun.

Ryann was fully awake now and quite positive that the dazzling aura facing him from in front of his window was not the hall light from his parents entering the bedroom. Golden hues flowed out of the whiteness, showering itself on everything in the room. It reminded Ryann of sprinkles of pixie dust in some of his favorite childhood books. His blue eyes grew wide trying to capture the unbelievable event unfolding before him.

"Fear not, Ryann," a confident, yet kind, voice began. "I have come to do the bidding of one much greater than I and who you have found favor with."

Rapid pulses in his chest gripped Ryann as he struggled to understand what was happening. Instinctively he grasped his navy blue bed sheets and pulled them up so that only his eyes and the top of his head peeked out from his self-made cocoon. Squinting to reduce the brilliance before him, Ryann stared into the light, trying to detect a form while questions scrambled around his mind. What had the voice meant by "finding favor," and who had sent him? As Ryann struggled to work this out, the center of the whiteness began to take the shape of a man. Human in appearance, he looked powerful, but there was a calmness about his face, like that of an experienced commander before going into battle. Ryann recalled hearing about angels in his Sunday school class at church. He wondered if this could be one.

"Ryann, thou have found favor with the One who sent me. You will be given much and much will be required of you."

Still shaking, Ryann was fairly certain he was safe. "S-s-s...sir, are you an angel?"

"You have perceived correctly."

"And...I've been chosen by someone...for something?" Ryann asked.

"The One who knows you better than you know yourself," the angel answered.

Ryann knew he must be talking about God, but what could God possibly want with him?

"What am I supposed to do?"

"Thou must search out and put on the full armor of God so that you can take a stand against the devil's schemes. For your struggle is not against flesh and blood, but against the powers of this dark world and against the forces of evil in the heavenly realms."

"The devil? Forces of evil? I'm just a kid," Ryann said. "What could I possibly have to do with all of this? You've got to be making a mistake."

"There are no mistakes with God. Thou have heard of David?"

"You mean the David from David and Goliath?" Ryann asked.

The angel nodded. "He was also a boy chosen by God to accomplish great things. God chooses to show His power by using the powerless."

Ryann tried to comprehend the magnitude of what this mighty being was saying to him. Realizing he was still sitting in his bed, covers bunched around him, he pulled them aside and swung his feet out, never taking his eyes off the angel. Landing firmly on the carpet, Ryann's wobbly knees barely supported him, the bed acting as a wall between him and the angel.

"Who are you?"

"I am Gabriel and have come to give you insight and understanding."

"Wow!" Ryann couldn't believe this was the same angel who had appeared to Joseph and Mary in the Christmas story he heard every December. The lines of excitement on his face drooped as he fidgeted, thinking about the angel's words. "I don't want to…seem…ungrateful," Ryann hesitated, "but…is there any way you can…ask someone else?"

"Only you have been given this trial, Ryann, yet you shall not be alone."

"Who will help me?"

"As the young shepherd boy David spoke, 'The angel of the Lord encamps around those who fear Him, and He delivers them. For He commands His angels to guard you in all your ways.'" Gabriel's twinkling gaze rose as he stretched his arms heavenward, "And these will assist you along the way."

Beckoning Ryann from behind the bed, the angel glided effortlessly forward to greet him. Walking to within a foot of Gabriel, Ryann bowed humbly, basking in the radiant glow that emanated all around him. Reaching out, the angel grasped Ryann's left hand firmly and slipped a gold ring, topped by a clear bubble-like stone, onto his finger. Before he could inspect it, the angel took his other hand and placed a long metal pole in it. Ryann's hand slid easily up and down the smooth metal finish. Its shape and size were similar to a pool cue. Bone-white buttons protruded from just below where he gripped the staff. They were numbered 1, 2, 3, 4, 5, 6, and 7. Mesmerized by the gifts that begged for more attention and questions, Ryann hardly noticed Gabriel loop a long leather cord through his arm and around his neck. From it a curved ivory horn hung loosely below his waist, resting on his hip.

As Gabriel finished and backed away, Ryann continued marveling at each of the gifts. Reaching down to inspect the horn, he ran his hands along its smooth, yet pitted surface, until he reached the small gold-tipped opening. He wondered how old the horn was and if it had been used before.

"What do I do with these? How do I use them?"

"It is not for me to reveal," answered the angel calmly. "You shall find out in due time."

"But what do I do now?"

"Thou must seek the King's sword."

"How? What King? Where do I look?" Ryann blurted out, panicking as questions continued to pop into his head.

"The Spirit will lead you, and the ring will open the way," the angel replied as he began floating backwards, the light peeling away with him.

"Wait, wait! Don't leave—I don't know enough—where do I go now?"

"Remember," Gabriel's clear voice began to fade, "all Scripture is God-breathed and is useful for teaching, rebuking, correcting, and training in righteousness, so that you may be thoroughly equipped for all good works."

Clutching the mysterious heavenly gifts he had been given, Ryann collapsed in a heap on his bed, body and mind drained from his supernatural encounter. He drifted into a welcomed sleep.

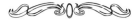

It seemed Drake's bedroom no longer existed. Only his bed remained, an island floating in a sea of darkness that completely surrounded him. His eyes bulged, darting about for anything that would give him a hint of what was going on. A cool draft drifted down his neck, chilling him despite the safety of his covers. Caught between reality and a nightmare, he let loose a scream that normally would have been heard throughout the house and beyond, but now was absorbed into the heavy darkness enveloping him.

"Who's there?" he said again. He pinched himself to see if he was dreaming.

With a loud *swooooooosh*, huge wings shot out of the darkness surrounding his bed. Drake dove for the safety of his covers.

A thunderous, commanding voice ordered, "Come out from hiding and stand up!"

Drake hesitated, knuckles tense and white as they curled tightly around the edges of his blanket.

"*Now!*" the voice thundered.

Jerking his covers off, Drake scurried to the edge of the bed, lost his balance, and awkwardly fell face-first onto the cool floor. Petrified at what he might see, yet too scared to disobey, he raised his head slightly. Half expecting some hideous beast, Drake was surprised at what he was facing. The black-winged warrior towering over him was imposing enough to paralyze anyone with fear, but his face was what captivated Drake. Instead of a hideous three-eyed ghoul with fangs, like Drake imagined, he stared into one of the most ruggedly handsome faces he had ever seen. Drake froze, mesmerized.

"Sit up and listen closely, human," the dark angel began, closing his wings in an effortless swish. Lowering his voice, he spoke in a precise, but less threatening tone. "I have chosen you to carry out my wishes."

Drake raised himself to a clumsy crouch. The face he looked intently into was perfect in almost every way, except for a long thin scar that traveled from his left ear to his jaw. He was convinced now that this wasn't a monster trying to devour him.

"Why me?"

The angel's scar became more noticeable when he smiled at Drake. "I have been here before with great success and have reason to believe you will serve me well."

"What do you want me to do?" Drake blurted.

"The one who seeks to bind me must be stopped!"

Drake stumbled backwards, putting a hand on the floor to keep from falling. Swallowing hard, he could feel the black, penetrating eyes staring deep into his.

"You are the one," the creature said confidently.

No one had ever chosen Drake for anything, yet this powerful being wanted him. He didn't know if he could trust the dark angel or not, but the chance for power excited Drake. "How do I do it?"

The dark angel continued to smile, sensing the blackness in Drake's heart spreading murkily throughout his body.

"I will be your eyes and ears, a guide to lead you in the right direction, and," he hesitated, "I will give you these."

The dark-winged angel stretched out his hand, his index finger pointing toward the empty floor in front of him. Immediately three items appeared before Drake's eyes. He blinked again. They were still there. Drake's hand shot out in a blur to grab the closest item.

"Stop!"

Drake froze, and then cowered, his eyes shifting back to the booming voice as he slowly retracted his hand. His eyes darted back and forth between the three items and the dark angel in the awkward silence.

"You move when I tell you to move. Now...kneel before me, child of the earth, while I make you ready for your task."

Still hunched-over, Drake pitched forward onto his knees with his head bowed, eyes glancing upward in anticipation.

"My first gift to you is a cloak of darkness. It will provide you with cover at night. You and the night shall become one."

Drake reached out his hands to receive the cloak. It felt smooth and slippery. Looking intently at it, the cloak seemed several feet thick, as if it was projecting darkness.

"My second gift to you is a ring of suggestion. With it you will have the ability to project persuasive thoughts to those who are weak-willed or in the midst of indecision."

Powerful hands with long curled fingers took hold of Drake's hand, spreading an icy chill from the tip of his fingers to his wrist. As the creature slipped the black band onto his finger, Drake briefly noticed a red blotch on the top. His hand felt stiff, then the numbness traveled up his arm and throughout his body. Chattering clicks from his own teeth broke the silence as he awaited the angel's next words.

"Lastly, I provide you with a bow and arrows of fire. These arrows were formed in the lake of fire and will deliver physical and mental anguish to those they touch."

"Thank you…uhh…what should I call you?" Drake asked.

"I am one of the stars that fell from heaven. My master is Shandago and I am his chief messenger. You may call me Lord Ekron."

"Thank you, Lord Ekron, for these gifts. I may be young, but I'll do as you ask to the best of my ability."

"It is expected. Also, these items I have given to you are not for use in this world. When the time is right, you will find a passage into another land. There you will put these gifts to work."

The darkness in the room began to rush toward Lord Ekron, as if he were absorbing it, except he wasn't getting bigger—only darker. Drake kept staring at him, trying not to blink, so he wouldn't miss anything. Despite his efforts, the dark angel began to fade, and Drake found himself peering into the darkness at the blank wall. When he was sure his eyes weren't playing tricks on him and enough time passed so that he felt safe to move, he stood up.

Drake would have thought this was all a bad dream, but the items he held in his hand were proof that it was real. He ran his hands through the dense blackness of the slick cloak, wondering how he might use it. Drake was anxious to try the bow and arrows as well. He didn't dare pull the arrows out of their quiver right now, but decided that he would have to buy a regular bow and quiver of arrows as soon as possible so that he could begin practicing. Looking down at his hand, he examined the unusual ring he now wore. The entire band was a glossy black, except for the unusual red marking on the top, which resembled a flying dragon.

Not much had gone right for Drake during the first thirteen years of his life. "Now things are going to be different," he thought. The smile inching across his face looked evil. He knew with Lord Ekron at his side no one would be able to tell him what to do.

CHAPTER 2

Friends for Life

OUNT DORA WAS a small town full of budding memories waiting to blossom. It reminded visitors of the place where they grew up, or wished they had. "New England" in its style, the town was a mixture of quaint streets, charming bed and breakfast inns, and a wide variety of unique specialty and antique shops. Majestic palms and sprawling palmetto bushes were the only clues that it wasn't Vermont or Rhode Island. That and the weather, of course. Most of America was stifling hot and sticky in the summer. This cozy lakeshore village, tucked away about thirty miles northwest of bustling Orlando, Florida, was hot and humid six or seven months of the year. Late fall through early spring brought a short reprieve from the heat, which also brought more tourists.

Ryann smiled whenever he thought about how lucky he was that his parents decided to leave the big city five years ago when he was only seven. Right away, the kids in his class had befriended him. At home his stomach ached from all the freshly baked pies and cookies the neighborhood ladies brought over. It reminded Ryann of a place to drop Tom Sawyer and Huckleberry Finn so they could continue their spirited and carefree adventures. What impressed Ryann the most, though, were all the ways to get around town. There were cars and bicycles like any other town, but there were also trolleys and horse-drawn carriages. Best of all were the restored trains that circled the town on the hour.

Soon after his family moved in, Ryann decided that Mount Dora was a funny name for the town. It wasn't built on the top or side of a mountain, although for Florida, it was rather hilly. Friendly folks at the Chamber of Commerce told tourists that Dora Drawdy and her family had come down from Georgia in the 1840s to settle on the small ridge above what later was named Lake Dora by surveyors. At 184 feet above sea level, Mount Dora qualified as a mount or small hill, not a mountain. It amused Ryann to think that Dora had named it that as a way of playing a joke on gullible Northerners.

Resting on the north shores of Lake Dora, a large fishing and boating lake, Mount Dora was sectioned off into a small grid of shops and homes. Fifth Avenue and Donnelly Street crisscrossed, providing the major thoroughfare for local traffic and tourists. Donnelly Street flowed from uptown down to the water's edge at Evans Park, and Fifth Avenue split it halfway in between.

Some aspects of the small town were just like any other. There were the simple white planked or red brick churches every few blocks, the local grocer and fire station, and, of course, one elementary, middle, and high school each. Other aspects of the town lent themselves to spur Ryann's imagination. Stores with names like Piglet's Pantry, Memories and Marvels, The Painter's Daughter, and the intriguing Goblin Market. Burnt-red brick alleyways provided enticing hideaways and secret shortcuts, while just below town, brown steel tracks from the Florida Central Railroad cradled Lake Dora's sleepy shoreline.

"Get up, sleepyhead, we've got to get ready for church," the melodious voice of his mother sang.

"Mmm…yeah…okay," Ryann mumbled, flipping over on his stomach, eyes clamped shut and hair tussled about like grass runners searching for new soil. You could set your watch by the precise military-like routine that occurred every Sunday morning in the Watters's house—the 7:30 wake-up call, then showering, dressing, and being seated for breakfast by 8:15. Ryann's mother wasn't a short-order cook, but she made sure his favorites—a bowl of cinnamon-apple oatmeal, two halves of bagel, one with cream cheese, the other with peanut butter, and a glass of orange juice—were waiting at his spot when he rolled lazily down the stairs to the kitchen.

"Good morning, Ryann," his mother smiled. "Sleep well?"

"Yes, ma'am," he replied, while thinking to himself, "if you consider being visited by an angel, given special gifts, and told to find a King's sword, sleeping well."

"Just great," he muttered, grinning to himself, as a rumble from the stairs announced his brother and sister bounding down. Their black-and-white border collie, Pepper, yipped at their heels, bringing him out of his trance.

"Beat'cha!" Alison cheered, dashing into her chair. Her juice splashed over the side of her glass as she jarred the table. Ryann rolled his eyes.

"Big deal," said Henry Jr. He tried to act as if he didn't care, but Ryann knew he did. Henry never wanted anyone to beat him at anything, especially their sister.

Looking up from his paper, their father warned, "Okay kids, let's eat up and get on our way. We don't want to be late for church." He drew the ritual to a close by cinching up his tie as he sat down to a bowl of his favorite cereal.

Ryann swallowed the second bite of his peanut butter bagel, but didn't feel hungry anymore. Racing down to breakfast, he had left the staff out on his bed and didn't want anyone in his family to discover it. His chair screeched as he pushed back from the table.

"Ryann, you hardly touched anything this morning," his mother noticed.

"Uhh...yes, ma'am...I guess I'm just not hungry this morning," Ryann answered as he offered his food to his brother before racing up the stairs.

Ryann often thought being the second of three kids caused him to fight harder for his parents' attention. "That might work to my advantage now," he reasoned as he hid the angel's gifts in his closet. Grabbing his Bible off the shelf, he raced back downstairs and outside to the car. His father had the engine running and was staring at his watch as if fearful it might try to run away. Ryann laughed to himself. Without looking down at his own watch, he knew it was 8:45 on the dot.

The First Presbyterian Church of Mount Dora sat atop a hilly slope just off Fifth Avenue, overlooking the lake. Most Northerners felt comfortable in its traditional New England construction. The outside was brick with white trim, while four sturdy white pillars shouldered the outer foyer and steeple. Founded in 1960, it was much newer than most of the historic churches in town, but Ryann's father had won the brief debate over which church they would attend, preferring what he called "practical Bible teaching" over historical significance.

Ryann was thankful Sunday school hour was first. He couldn't wait to share his secret with his best friends, Terell and Liddy.

"Guys, you'll never believe what happened to me last night!" Ryann blurted out. With a whoosh he slid into the seat saved between them.

His excitement grabbed their attention as Mrs. Gigabund, her twenty-pound black Bible in hand, shuffled into the room.

"Let's meet outside on the sidewalk before going into morning service," Ryann said. The loud *whomp* from Mrs. Gigabund's family Bible crashing down on her desk signified the start of class. Jumping in his seat along with eleven other sixth graders, Ryann made a mental note to watch next time and see from how high she actually dropped that thing. Mrs. Gigabund folded her meaty hands neatly on the front of her ankle-length skirt. Looking around the class, her marshmallow face gleamed brightly. Ryann imagined that's what she'd look like if she'd just won first prize in the county fair pie-baking contest. Clearing her throat, Mrs. Gigabund began the week's lesson. Ryann didn't hear a word. He found himself staring out the window, reliving last night's encounter with Gabriel.

The double white doors that led from the church basement out to McDonald Street shot open as Ryann bounded out. Scurrying over to the sidewalk, he stumbled over the long legs of someone seated on the lone shaded bench. "Excuse me…uh…sir," Ryann stuttered, a light pink rising in his ears.

"That's quite all right, young man," the calm voice replied.

Ryann didn't recall a park bench here before and wondered what the thinly gray-haired man was doing. In his worn and rumpled suit, Ryann guessed he was a bum trying to dress up in his Sunday best.

"What's your name?" Ryann asked, figuring it was okay to talk to strangers on Sunday, especially if they were seated in the shadows of the church.

"Most folks call me Old Man Johnson. Real name's Noah Johnson. You can call me Noah."

"Nice to meet you, Mist—" Ryann caught himself, "Noah." Noah grinned back at him.

"Well, I have to go meet some friends now," Ryann said as he turned to walk away.

He took a few steps then turned back around. "Oh, I'm sorry, my name's Ryann, Ryann Watters."

Ryann watched Noah nod and tip his hat, his unusually bright blue eyes sparkling back at him. As he turned to race away and meet Liddy and Terell, Ryann thought he heard Noah mutter, "I know."

"That's silly," he thought, shaking his head. Looking up the street to the corner, Ryann saw Liddy and Terell heading around the side of the church, from letting their parents know where they were going before the service.

"Hey guys! Down here!" Ryann yelled to his friends.

"Wha... what's the big deal?" Terell asked eagerly. Since the day Ryann had met Terell, he had stuttered whenever he was excited or afraid. A lot of kids would make fun of it, but Ryann didn't care and the two quickly had become friends.

Ryann summarized the previous night's events, realizing they had to get back into the church service. Terell and Liddy's mouths gaped open until the end. Terell's closed first.

"Is this another one of your jokes, Ryann?" he asked.

"No, no joke, we've got to get together this afternoon so I can give you more of the details. Let's meet at the park at two o'clock sharp."

Terell and Liddy laughed, "Is there anything else besides 'sharp' for a Watters?" Terell asked.

"We'll be there!" Liddy chipped in.

Ryann sat waiting in the gazebo in Evans Park. He looked at his watch for the fourth time, tapping his foot on the hard cedar deck. Quiet except for the constant humming of locusts, the park jutted out into Lake Dora at the end of Donnelly Street. Looking out over the choppy blue-green water, Ryann gazed at the familiar sight of families backing their boats in at the public ramps across the inlet. The red-and-white striped lighthouse, a gift to the city in the late 1980s, was one of the town's major landmarks.

"Yo, Ryann!" the silence was broken by Terell as Liddy and he came pedaling up on their bicycles.

"Hope you weren't waiting long," Liddy added as they came to a stop. Her real name was Lydia Thomas. Lydia was a family name handed down from her great-grandmother, but she preferred Liddy and everyone but her parents introduced her that way. Since Ryann first met Liddy, he admired her for her feisty spirit and rock-solid confidence. She wasn't snooty, but Ryann didn't know many sixth graders, or seventh- or eighth-graders for that matter, who would take her on in a battle of wits.

Ryann reviewed all the action of the previous night, trying hard not to leave out any details, but wanting to get it all out as quickly as he could. Exhaling deeply when he finished, Ryann looked back and forth between his friends, "Well?" he asked hesitantly.

Liddy spoke up first, "Boy, Ryann, you've got quite an imagination." She shook her head.

Ryann turned his attention to Terell, who stayed silent, avoiding his pleading gaze.

"You guys are supposed to be my best friends." Ryann winced momentarily then puffed out his chest and raised his voice, "Well, what do you have to say about this?" Fishing into the front pocket of his blue jeans, he pulled out the bubble-stone ring.

"Ah!" Ryann jerked his hand away as if the ring were a hot iron, watching it fall and bounce on the wooden deck. Terell and Liddy both jumped back. The ring had been clear, but was now emitting a bright blue glow.

On the Northeast side of town, about two miles away and close to the middle school, Drake Dunfellow had just finished mowing the patchy thin grass in his front yard. The old push mower sputtered to a halt as spiraling dust from the parched sandy soil settled on the rusty metal body.

"Drake! Whatcha stoppin' for, boy? There's a whole nuther halfa yard to mow." The raspy voice came from the deep shadows within the metal shed. Drake saw the craggy nose appear first. As long as he could remember, Uncle Simon had that sinister look about him. Maybe it was his hook nose. Or perhaps it was his dark eyes that were tied so closely together. More than likely it was the bushy eyebrows connecting at the bridge of his nose. They rose up sharply, and then reversed direction downward to the edge of his eyes. "Like bats," Drake thought.

Uncle Simon Dunfellow was the oldest brother of Drake's father. Following the death of Drake's parents in a car crash when he was six, his aunt and uncle were the only relatives who stepped forward to take him in. Many nights after he first arrived, Drake cried himself to sleep. Even at six, he had fond thoughts of laughing together, tenderhearted bear hugs, and the reassuring words of "I love you" from his parents. Slowly, over time, his aunt and uncle chased the good memories away and replaced them with thoughts of greed, resentment, and intimidation. Uncle Simon and Aunt Belial never had any children of their own, and Drake always thought it was probably a good thing. Drake felt like their servant, relied on for all the chores and heavy work around the house. When it came to holidays, special presents, or fancy vacations, he didn't have anything to talk about like the other kids at school. He usually resorted to making things up.

"I'll get to it, Uncle. I need a water break first."

"When I was a youngster," Uncle Simon began, hands on his hips and pointy jaw sticking out, "we use ta work all day in the blazin' sun pickin' limes." He cocked his head to the side as if bringing back the yesteryears. "Thorns dug inta our arms till we bled, an' we never asked for water till the end of the day... an' we liked it."

Drake thought he was nuts. "Well, I'm gettin' some water!" He stormed into the dilapidated house, letting the wooden door slam and bounce back off the frame.

Drake grabbed a cup out of the laminated cupboard, flipped the stained handle on the tap up, and let the water run until it was slightly cooler than room temperature. All the while he kept his eyes focused on the back of his gray-haired Aunt Belial, who was rocking back and forth hypnotically in the antique rocker on the rickety back porch. She was worse than her husband, if there could be such a thing. Retracing his steps through the house, the hairs on his neck stood on end anticipating her voice.

"Have a good sleep last night, Sonny?" Drake hated her using the name Sonny, but he wasn't about to tell her so. Not here. Not now.

"Uh, yeah, fine," he got out quickly, his uneasiness fading the farther away he got from her.

Aunt Belial continued her slow rocking, the feeble chair creaking with each movement. She didn't have to see her young nephew's face to know that she made him nervous; Drake's rapid steps from the kitchen to the front door confirmed it. "This boy has promise," she thought as the chair continued creaking. Her eyes darkened as her upper lip quivered slightly, one corner turning upward in a sinister grin.

Ryann tentatively bent over to pick up the ring. Examining it closely, he decided it was safe and slipped it on his finger. Looking up at his two astonished friends, he asked, "Would you like me to get the other stuff?"

"OK...OK...who's a jerk, raise your hand," Terell moaned as Liddy and he raised their hands in surrender together. Ryann knew it was tough for Liddy to admit.

"Is it magic?" she asked, amazed, but still maintaining some distance.

"Come on Liddy, you know magic isn't real—this is supernatural!"

"So what now?" She eyed the ring suspiciously.

"I don't know," Ryann answered, "I guess I'm waiting for instructions."

"Didn't the angel…what'd you say the dude's name was?" Terell asked.

"Gabriel."

"Didn't Gabriel," Terell continued, "give you any clues on what to do next, besides 'find the sword'?"

"Well…" Ryann shut his eyes tightly, "as he was drifting away, he did tell me that 'All scripture was God-breathed' and that it is 'useful' for all sorts of things." His voice rose in excitement as his eyes popped open, "And he said that I would be 'thoroughly equipped' by using it!"

"That, that's it!" Terell cried out. "You just…just need to look in your Bible to see what to do next."

"But how do I know where to look?"

"Listen Ryann," Terell said, calming down. "Do I need to do all the work around here? I don't know, just go home, open it up, and see what happens. Maybe that ring of yours will help."

Enthused about the possibilities, the three friends headed home on their bikes. Terell and Ryann split off together down McDonald Street to their neighborhood, while Liddy continued along the breezy shore to her house on the lake. Squinting behind his circular wire-rim glasses, the sun reflecting brightly off his dark brown skin, Terell chased his best friend into their subdivision. Ryann skidded into Terell's driveway first, coming to a halt just in time to turn and see his friend pressing his foot down to come to a hard stop.

"Beat'cha again!" Ryann laughed in a way that was taken as good ribbing from a best friend. Being in the same grade and living just around the corner from one another, it was inevitable that the two had become friends. Ryann recalled Terell moving in a little more than two years ago. At first he was shocked to hear some of the stories Terell would tell about growing up in downtown Atlanta in a predominately black neighborhood called Vine City. It was a tough part of town near the Georgia Dome, and when Terell's aunt died suddenly and left a house to his mother in Mount Dora, it didn't take much for her to get out and start over. His mother was able to continue her teaching career at Mount Dora High School, and despite leaving friends behind in "The Bluff," Terell was excited to have less stress in a small town. His mother had even commented to Ryann that every month he was stuttering less and less. Initially Ryann had felt sorry for him not knowing his father or having any siblings, but in a short period of time they had become like brothers.

Resting just off Eleventh Street, a well-traveled thoroughfare from uptown to the lake, the cozy, close-knit subdivision, The Highlands of Mount Dora, included twenty-five houses. Typical of small town suburbia, the yards and homes were tidy and well maintained.

"Give me a call if you find out anything new," Terell shouted as Ryann pedaled away from the white, one-story ranch house with the bright green shutters. "You'll be the first to know," Ryann shouted back.

He turned the corner and raced into the cul-de-sac. The front door of his two-story house, a plum purple at his mother's insistence, stared back at him. Ryann coasted down their snake-like driveway, sloping around to the garage. Thick woods covered the pitched backyard that eventually ran down to a small pond. Running up the steps from the garage to the kitchen, Ryann burst through the door.

"Hey, Mom!"

Even in his haste, passing through the kitchen to the next flight of stairs, Ryann caught a whiff of his favorite sauce sizzling on the stove. "Fish tonight," he thought, as he hit the first step.

"Wash up, Ryann, we're going to eat in just a few minutes," his mom called out without turning around.

Ryann raced through dinner as quickly as he could and abruptly excused himself so he could get back to his room. Grabbing the Bible he had been given by the church following graduation from his sixth grade catechism class, Ryann almost tore the delicate pages opening to the index. He quickly read down the names of the sixty-six books—nothing jumped out at him. "Hmm, I wonder where I should start?" Resting his ring hand on top of the Bible and expecting something miraculous to happen, he waited. Still nothing. The blue glow had long since departed and was replaced by its normal clear color.

"Ryann? Are you done with your homework?" His mom's nightly question resounded up the stairwell.

"Gettin' to it, Mom!" Ryann shouted, returning the Bible to the shelf and picking up his schoolbooks. "How's a guy supposed to do homework when he has an angel giving him important business to carry out?" Ryann muttered to himself.

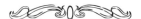

The morning sunshine peeked its orange and yellow head over solemn oaks in The Highlands as Ryann rolled to a stop in front of Terell's house. Except for a lone Friday this year when he woke up with a fever, the two hadn't missed a day of biking to school together. After crossing through one stoplight at the corner of Eleventh and Donnelly, it was a straight shot, about five blocks over, to Highland Street and a quick sprint up to school.

"Find anything?" Terell half-whispered through the early morning silence cast over their quiet neighborhood.

"Nah...not a thing," Ryann answered.

"You gonna wear the ring to school?"

"Yeah, you never know what might happen. I better have it close to me just in case. Come on, let's go. We're gonna be late!" The two sped off together, not realizing that today would be the beginning of countless challenging adventures and a friendship that would soon be put to the test.

CHAPTER 3

Into the World Beyond

"**H**EY! CUT IT out!" the smaller boy cried, glancing around, hoping that his shout would draw the attention of others. His neck still stung from Drake's open-handed slap.

"Loser," Drake spat, labeling his unfortunate classmate while making his way to his seat in the back of the room.

Drake Dunfellow knew that no one cared much for him— which was like saying no one wants to get poked in the eye with a stick. Unless, of course, they were out on the ball field choosing teams, then everyone wanted him on their team. They just had to be more concerned about winning than having fun. Drake should have been in the seventh grade—for his age, not his smarts—but had repeated first grade the year he came to live with his aunt and uncle. Clearly taller than the rest of the boys in class, this extra year of growth had him not only towering over everyone, but easily outweighing them as well.

"All you are is a bully," the smaller boy squeaked while everyone looked on.

"Thanks," Drake said with a sly smile, "I'll take that as a compliment."

For a small-town school, Mount Dora Middle School was surprisingly run down. Having grown up around it with older brothers and sisters attending, the kids there now didn't seem to notice, but the home of the Eagles had seen better days. Built in the 1960s, the beige and dusty yellow block buildings were intermixed with temporary trailers on cinderblocks. Weeds sprouted haphazardly across broken pavement on the outdoor basketball court, on which one of the four rims was missing. Air conditioning units stuck their ugly heads out of each classroom window, dripping their slobber and stain marks on anything beneath them. All of the six hundred sixth- through eighth-graders loved the place and had pride in the Eagles, due mostly to moving on from elementary school, not the fancy buildings or fresh paint.

"Did you find out anything new about the ring?" Liddy blurted out as she slid into her desk next to Ryann and Terell in their first period language arts class.

"Shh," they both hissed sharply, their heads swiveling around like radar to see who might be listening. Eager chatter from the other students filled the background.

"Nothing's changed at all," Ryann muttered, talking out of the corner of his mouth. "And it's obviously not blue anymore." He held it up to show her.

"What's going on here?" a familiar sarcastic voice interrupted. Ryann's shoulder sank under the pressure of a weighty hand. "Anything I should know about?"

"Why, no, Drake, unless of course you're interested in joining our debate on creation versus evolution," Liddy chided with her sweetest voice.

Terell sat motionless, hoping the big lug wouldn't look his way.

"So, Drake…are you more Darwinian or theistic in your beliefs?" Liddy pressed, fluttering her eyelashes at him.

"Huh?" Drake looked back at her dumbfounded for a moment, eyes narrowing while his fingers dug deep into Ryann's shoulder, "Aww, shut up!" He sneered and lumbered away much more slowly than he had appeared.

"Jeez, thanks, Liddy." Ryann rubbed his throbbing shoulder. "What in the world were you talking about?"

"Oh! Just something I've been reading up on in my free time. Too bad you couldn't see the look on his face, Ryann." She giggled. "It was like I was speaking a foreign language to him."

"As far as I'm concerned, you were," Ryann beamed, both proud at her quick thinking and impressed again with her pursuit of knowledge.

Ryann turned to address his somber friend. "You okay, Terell?"

"Ya, ya, yeah…I'm, I'm alright," Terell stuttered, his heart still racing from the brief encounter. "Drake ju…just reminds me of this bad dude that used to cruise our hood."

"Seats, everyone…it's time for class." Ms. Buttlework's comical nasal voice drew everyone's attention. In her fifties and never married, Ms. Buttlework's life was teaching kids. Ryann watched until the graying, pudgy teacher waddled over to the board and began to write the lesson for the day on the board.

"After school at the fishin' hole," Ryann whispered to Terell as he reached down to pull his homework out of his book bag.

At least twice a week, the two friends would get permission to drop by their favorite fishing hole after school and try their luck before going home. Today was one of those days.

Lake Franklin was the perfect spot for bass fishing as far as Ryann and Terell were concerned. It was eight blocks down Highland Street to one of the five traffic lights in town, onto Fifth Street, then left past the high school and down the hill. Liddy rarely went with them because her mother drove her to and from school. Living at least a mile farther away than both Ryann and Terell, driving was both quicker and safer. And Liddy was on the soccer team, which took up a lot of her time after school.

"I'm gonna catch old Fred today, I can feel it," Terell yelled over the wind racing across his closely shaved, curly black hair as the two coasted down the hill to a dirt road that veered off to the left. Ryann pulled up alongside his friend after letting him lead for a change. "Fred" was their nickname for the biggest bass they had ever seen in Lake Franklin. Over time it had grown to mythical proportions whenever they talked about it.

"Oh, yeah, I think Fred's a little too smart to be caught by you," Ryann kidded. They came to a stop, got off their bicycles, and walked them up into the thick brush out of sight from the main road.

Thick beams of light poured through the canopied treetops that did their best to shut out the invading light. Walking around the rope-like vines that wrapped together like military cargo nets, the boys made their way through broad, heart-shaped plants surrounding the small woods. This was where they came during fall football games to sneak up the hill and under the chain-link fence that surrounded the Mount Dora High School football field. They convinced themselves it was okay not to pay as long as they snuck in after the game had started. Fall was still a long way off, though, and landing the biggest bass was what captivated both of their minds now. Ryann laughed to himself as they passed the No Swimming sign. It was so over-

grown with vines and leaves you would need to have seen it
when they first started fishing there years ago to know what it
said. Hopping over the downed telephone pole that kept cars
from pulling forward any further, Terell broke the silence, "So,
do you think Drake heard anything we said this morning about
Gabriel or your ring?"

"Nah. He's so dense he wouldn't have made heads or tails of
it anyway," Ryann answered.

"Good, 'cuz I'd hate to have that big idiot givin' us problems."

The steady, rythmic hum of locusts surrounded the boys on
the walk to their favorite swimming hole. Dragonflies hovered
and jerked in erratic spurts on either side of the winding trail.
Fortunately, someone in the surrounding neighborhood had
been kind enough to cut a rough path through the tall, dense
grass that encircled the undeveloped side of the lake.

"Ryann! Look at your ring!" Terell shouted. Ryann peered
down at his hand as if it didn't belong to him. The familiar blue
had returned. Goose bumps sprouted up and down his arm,
followed by a quick chill.

"It's gotta be because of the water," Ryann reassured himself
and Terell as the initial shock began to fade.

"Take a few steps back," Terell directed, conducting his own
little experiment. Ryann backed up, first three steps, then four,
and the ring began to fade to its normal clear color. Walking
forward again, it slowly began turning blue.

"That's it!" Ryann exclaimed.

"The ring must change colors based upon what's around or, I
guess, depending on where I am, because I'm wearing it."

"Cool," Terell said, "I wonder if it only turns blue or if it
changes to other colors, too."

"Guess we'll have to wait and see," Ryann speculated aloud,
reaching behind the thick, weedy grass where they kept their
cane poles hidden.

Terell scanned the murky waters, minnows clearly visible
swimming innocently near the shallow, sandy banks. Just a few

feet out, the muddy brown waters created the perfect cover for the big bass minnow eaters.

"Let's go out to the island," Terell suggested, "I think they'll be bitin' out there today."

They sauntered around to one of three small inlets that connected to form Lake Franklin. The land out there wasn't really an island, but they liked to pretend it was. It was actually a peninsula that jutted out into the middle of the small lake.

Crack! Ryann snapped one of the craggy, dead sticks that jutted up both in and around the lake. That was one of the biggest challenges of Lake Franklin, not just catching a fish, but doing it without getting caught on all the debris.

"This looks good," Terell said, and plopped down on the brittle grass. Both boys had quickly grown used to the soft blue glow emanating from Ryann's right hand. Now it was time to settle in for the fisherman's wait. Some call it boring, but for those who like to fish, it held those rare peaceful moments when everything in the background gradually became noticeable. Both boys scanned the muddy water, flat as a table except for the occasional splash of a jumping fish. The only other movement was the whispering trees, barely stirring in a soft breeze. Surveying the thumbnail sketch of nature surrounding him, Ryann was still baffled why God would be so interested in him that He'd send a mighty angel like Gabriel to deliver the message.

"Do you ever wonder if God has everything figured out, or do you think He just gets involved in our lives when He feels like it?" Ryann pondered, casting his line out in front of him again.

"Whattaya mean?"

"You know, do you think He knew He was going to send Gabriel to visit me hundreds of years ago, or did He just decide to do it in the last few weeks?"

"Mmm, I don't know." Terell continued to stare off across the lake. A sudden twitch in his line distracted him.

"I mean, if He's God over all things, surely nothing happens without Him knowing about it or planning it, right?"

"Well, I think—" Terell began but never finished his answer, "Ryann! *Look at your ring!*"

Ryann gazed at the shimmering gold now pulsing from the ring. He dropped his pole.

"Wha...what do you suppose it means?" Terell asked, his nervous stutter kicking into high gear.

Ryann glanced about looking for what the golden glow was detecting. "If blue means water, what does gold mean?" he thought.

"There must be something around here somewhere," Ryann concluded. "Maybe it's treasure!"

On the other side of the lake, something moved where Ryann and Terell had left their bikes. Ryann was the first to notice it out of the corner of his eye. He dismissed it as the wind at first, before realizing the surface of the lake resembled a polished stone.

"Terell, get down," he whispered urgently through clenched teeth. He pressed down on Terell's back until both their faces were flattened into the dry, hay-like grass. "I think I saw someone over by our bikes. Stay still and wait."

Lying in this position, Ryann didn't think anyone could see them, but he couldn't see anything either. Slowly, very slowly, he stretched out his neck, just peeking over the taller uncut grass beside them.

It was Drake!

"No use hiding, losers!" the grisly voice boomed. "I see ya out there!"

They remained still, not wanting to acknowledge his words and too dismayed to know what to do next.

"Wha...wha...what now?" Terell tried to whisper, remembering their morning encounter with Drake and hoping his friend had an answer.

"Nice bikes!" They heard the obnoxious voice bark again, quickly followed by the tinny clinking of metal and the familiar sound of bicycles crashing to the ground. Drake's raucous laughter filled the air, and both boys sank deeper into the grass, their hearts pounding. Terell's ebony skin shimmered with droplets of sweat. Scrunching up his face, he tried to keep his glasses from slipping farther down his nose.

Rapid ripples, like the sound of hundreds of tiny fish feeding on a lone piece of bread, diverted Ryann's attention back toward the lake. A small, roughly formed gold circle glowed brightly in the murky water just a few feet away. The little ripples continued pushing the circle outward.

"He, he...here he...he comes!" Terell finally spat out, his eyes focused on the large boy lumbering down the beaten path toward them.

"Come on, get up," Ryann said calmly, his attention diverted by the glowing bubble beside them.

"What?" Terell cried out in disbelief. He briefly tore his eyes from the inevitable confrontation to see what was distracting Ryann. Terell starred hypnotically at the stirring gold water, his mind pleading to glance back at Drake. Paralyzed with fear, his mouth opened, but no sound came out. The choppy center sparkled fiercely, like it was electrified.

"H-h-he's coming, Ryann!" Terell's frantic voice rose as he grabbed his friend's shirt and tugged to be sure he was listening.

Ryann shrugged free. "I'm going in."

"Wha...what do you mean, 'going in'?" Terell asked incredulously.

"I'm jumping into the water."

"I-i-in there?" Terell pointed.

"Yeah, I feel like that's where He wants me to go."

"He? He who? Dra...Dra, Drake's almost here. Ryann, help! Wha...what do we do?" Terell's head swiveled back and forth between Drake and Ryann like he was watching a tennis match. Drake, brow furrowed and fists clenched, continued his heavy strides onto the peninsula.

"What's going on here?" Drake blared. He was now only twenty feet away.

"Bye, Terellllllll!" Ryann's voice rang out as he hurled his body off the bank toward the center of the glittery gold circle. Terell and Drake watched in amazement. Everything seemed to be moving in slow motion. Ryann's hair splayed out in all directions as he flew through the air. His arms stretched out for balance, but his legs squeezed tightly together as he dropped into the golden swirl. As Ryann's feet penetrated the circle, he slid into the goo-like substance with only the slightest ripple. The further he sank, the more it looked like he was being sucked into it, or pulled in from the other end. Ryann's head, eyes wide-open, disappeared from view, then only his outstretched arms were visible, and finally his stiff fingers slipped beneath the surface.

Ryann didn't really know what had caused him to want to jump. It was as if an inner voice had commanded, "Jump!" and he had obeyed like a boot camp Marine to his drill sergeant. But it was more than that. He knew what it was like to have his conscience alert him about something. That was the sickening sensation in the pit of his stomach he felt whenever he chose to do something he knew was wrong. This was different. Wave after wave of soothing peacefulness washed over him—not the fear he would have expected from jumping into the murky waters of the lake. It was the same combination of awe and calm he felt when he was with Gabriel.

His body hung in the water, slowly descending as if a giant invisible hand were lowering him by the nape of his neck. Ryann had anticipated the familiar sensations of jumping into water—the rapid immersion, tingling cold rushing over his skin, a scattering splash, followed by the blinding veil of the soupy-brown lake. Instead, he had oozed into the Jell-O-firm substance, glancing back at the perplexed faces of Terell and Drake until the golden fluid swallowed his head. The two boys left on the bank stood riveted in place, jaws slack, arms dangling loosely at their sides. Caught in the midst of a dazzling glow, he looked around rather than tightly shutting his eyes. His body basked in the glittery illumination, while only a few feet away an invisible wall held back the gloomy lake water on every side. Feeling helpless, Ryann began repeating a Bible verse that came to mind: "Yea, though I walk through the valley of the shadow of death, I will fear no evil: for thou art with me."

His descent ended abruptly as a bouncy surface pressed against the heaviness of his body. Ryann's weight continued pressing down, stretching the boundary's limits until his feet finally poked through the rubbery sac that contained him like a human cocoon. Ryann's mind grappled with the odd sensation that the lower half of his body dangled in the air, while his upper half was held firmly by the clenching liquid. The bright glow remained and helped keep him from panicking. Hanging in the balance between two worlds, Ryann felt like the next bead of liquid in a giant eyedropper, being squeezed out into the unknown.

A few more inches and his feet touched something solid. Supporting his own weight on solid ground, the rest of Ryann's body was pushed out forcefully. He crumpled into a heap. "Ugh," he exhaled, sucking in big gulps of fresh air. He slowed down, realizing he wasn't as out of breath as he had expected to be after being under water so long.

"I couldn't have held my breath the whole time I was in there," he thought.

Light-headed and still feeling like someone was giving him a bear hug, Ryann began surveying his body to make sure he was okay. With only a cursory once-over, he could see what he sensed—the golden substance was meant for his protection. No harm had come to him. Ryann noticed his ring was clear again, but was more puzzled to find that he wasn't even wet.

Rich green grass, like a thick, deep pile carpet, cushioned him. Smooth and plush, it reminded Ryann of running his hands through his dog Pepper's plentiful, fluffy fur. He raised his head to glance about, then grasped the abundant, wavy grass with both hands to steady himself.

Looking around, nothing could have prepared Ryann for the magnificent palette of colors before him. Striking yellows, plum and violet purples, splashes of orange and red, dotted pale and hot pinks, all against a backdrop of deep blue skies fading gradually as they cascaded earthbound into a sea of mixed greens of trees, bushes, and grass. His nose tingled with the sweet perfumes of the multi-colored blossoming flowers and full, fruity leaves. A low groan rose from somewhere within him as Ryann opened his eyes and mouth wide in awe at the majestic artistry around him. Everything seemed so bountiful, alive, and thriving that he felt he could stick out his tongue and taste it.

The sights reminded him of a cross between the Garden of Eden and the Thomas Kinkade paintings his mother collected. Ryann blinked in amazement again and again at the overwhelming clarity of each flower, leaf, and blade of grass.

In the distance, he heard the rapid clamor of urgent waters rushing over and around rocks and boulders.

Something was lying in the grass nearby. He rose, stepped forward, then reached down to pick up two familiar-looking objects. The staff and horn looked just like his. "No way," Ryann whispered to himself, having left them both in his closet. Somehow they had been transported with him. Placing his arm and neck through the leather strap, Ryann shifted the ivory horn so it rested comfortably on his hip. Gripping the smooth metal shaft of the staff, his body stiffened as he gritted his teeth and glanced around at his surroundings. Ryann's options narrowed to heading toward the rushing waters in front of him or toward a clearing behind him.

Before he could decide which direction to go, the faint rustle and quiver of leaves from a row of thick bushes to his right caught his attention.

"Who's there?" Ryann called with the most forceful voice he could muster.

The leaves froze, with only the slightest breeze causing them to flutter. Staring into the bushes as hard as he could, the colors and details seemed to blur, like a child mixing finger paints on a clean white page. Ryann blinked rapidly to clear his vision, then squinted back into the bushes, wondering whether he had really seen anything at all.

Snap!

"Hey! Come on out. I know you're in there."

CHAPTER 4

Aeliana
and the Word

RYANN TOOK A stance like one of the fighters in his video games, holding his staff out to defend himself. It seemed like the right thing to do, despite the fact he had never had to fight anyone. He knew he had heard the crisp snap of a small twig, yet the bushes that had rustled before remained still.

"Come out peacefully and no one will get hurt," Ryann called out. Hopefully, whatever it was would be able to understand him or even be scared away by his voice. Rushing waters replaced the emptiness of his hollow words as Ryann waited, scanning the dense bushes in front of him.

Just when he was about to turn away, the bushes shook and a high voice behind them spoke out, "I'm coming out now. I won't bite or claw."

"Bite or claw?" Ryann thought. "I would hope not." Whoever was coming out certainly would have a little explaining to do. He watched intently as the thick bushes shook vigorously and began to part.

Ryann jumped back at the sight of the raccoon bustling out of the brush. He thought, "Whoever was coming out must have startled the poor creature. I wonder what this person looks like." Only the raccoon didn't run off as Ryann expected. It rose up on its haunches and stared right back at him with beady black eyes, cocking its head to the side.

"Shoo, shoo," Ryann said to the animal, shaking his staff at it while peering over its head at the now motionless bushes.

"Excuse me," the raccoon spoke up in the high-pitched voice, "but I thought you said no one would get hurt?"

Ryann jumped back, almost stumbling over himself as he backpedaled. "What? Who? Ya...you're a raccoon."

"That's true, but not a violent one. I said I wouldn't bite or claw, and I always keep my word."

"Bu...but, raccoons can't talk."

The raccoon stared back, bringing its head back straight and then tilting it to the other side. "Mmm, I've never heard that before. Every raccoon I know can talk."

"Well, they can't where I come from."

"That may well be true, but I'm proof positive that at least one raccoon here on Aeliana can talk."

"Aeliana? Is that where I am?" Ryann scratched his head with his free hand.

"It is, and forgive me, but I never properly introduced myself." The raccoon stepped forward. "My name is Raz."

As Ryann peered back at the creature's pleasant furry face, the corners of his mouth curved upward in a thin smile. He could now see the liveliness in Raz's eyes that revealed the intelligence behind them. "He speaks as well as I do," Ryann thought. Breaking away from his trance, Ryann noticed the familiar black-and-white markings that made up Raz's mask, reminding him that this really *was* a raccoon.

"My name's Ryann," he replied, flashing Raz a broad grin.

"What? What's so funny?" Raz asked in his chatty, high-pitched voice.

"Oh, I just think it's funny that I'm actually having a conversation with a raccoon."

"Well, I wouldn't exactly call this a conversation. We've exchanged some pleasantries and all, but—"

"Ha!" Ryann interrupted with a full-blown belly laugh.

"Now, there you go again."

"I can't help it. I'm sorry, Raz, but it's all so comical. In our world there's no such thing as a talking animal, and, well, here I'm not only talking with one, but one with proper manners and vocabulary to boot."

Raz reached up with one of his slim paws and scratched the top of his head. After a brief pause, he spoke. "I suppose that could be funny to you. For me it's not quite the same, since there are a few human-like beings here on Aeliana."

"There are? Where are they?" Ryann asked

"Most of them prefer to live in Myraddin."

"What's Myraddin?"

"It's a castle and village on a hill overlooking the mouth of the three rivers."

"Amazing." Ryann shook his head.

"What?"

"All of this. I mean, just a few minutes ago I was fishing with my best friend and now I'm here," Ryann answered, turning around in a circle to emphasize his point.

"I'm sure it's because of the Word," Raz chimed in.

"The Word? What's the Word?"

"The Word is hard to explain," Raz answered. "Follow me."

With that, Raz turned, dropped down on all fours, and scurried off down a well-worn path. Ryann stared at him until the raccoon stopped, turned around, and with a twitch of his nose squeaked, "Come on!"

Bounding off after Raz, Ryann quickly realized he would have to move quicker than a brisk walk to keep up with him.

"Hey! Don't lose me," Ryann called out.

Raz stopped and turned around periodically to make sure Ryann was still following, but he kept up his scampering pace. His nose and ears still tingling with the enchanting smells and noises in the forest, Ryann wanted to look around, but he could only focus on Raz and the path in front of him if he didn't want to get lost. His heart pounded as the forest shadows began to part. Ryann squinted as a bright, gaping hole like the exit from a cave opened up in the trees. Rushing through the opening, he almost tripped over Raz, who sat on his haunches staring out in front of him.

"Gee whiz, Raz, you could have slowed up a little," Ryann said, between labored gasps.

The raccoon put his brown paw up to his mouth in the universal sign for quiet and then pointed in front of him.

On the precipice of a small mountain, Ryann and Raz looked out over a heavenly sight. The roar of thundering waters cascading over the side of the mountain into a lake far below was the focal point of this natural masterpiece. Circling the lake were trees of varying colors, shapes, and sizes. Splashes of grassy meadows dotted the forest as Ryann looked further out on the horizon. Far off on another hill, he thought he could make out the outline of a castle.

Ryann had many questions, the first of which Raz answered without being asked. "Yes, that's Myraddin you see off in the distance. Just north of that are the Joynnted Knolls. On the other side of the castle lies the great desert, and to the south are the Marrow Mountains."

"Awesome," Ryann whispered.

"Mmm…His work is beautiful, but only the Word is awesome," Raz replied, still staring straight ahead.

"There you go again. What is this Word thing?"

"In the beginning was the Word," Raz began. "All that you see is by His grand design."

"Why do you call Him 'The Word'?" Ryann asked.

Raz turned, his head bobbing up and down excitedly as he looked directly into Ryann's eyes. "He is the Author of life, the Beginning and the End, and He speaks to those who will listen. Once a year He speaks to us at Castle Myraddin."

"Whoa!" Ryann exclaimed, looking down at his hand. The clear bubble on his ring was now a shiny white glow.

"What does that mean?" Raz asked.

"I don't know. It glows blue when I'm near water, and it was gold just before I found the entrance to Aeliana. It started glowing white while you were talking."

"I'll stop talking and we'll see what happens." Raz turned to leave. "Follow me."

"Okay, but let's take it a little slower this time."

The ring went clear as Ryann fell in behind Raz and followed the jittery creature back into the forest on a different path. As they descended for quite some time, the ground leveled out and the trees slowly thinned until they came to the edge of a large, grassy meadow.

"We can talk just ahead," Raz said. "There's something I'd like to show you."

Melodious sounds from a scattered choir of birds filled the air as they continued in silence, traipsing across the meadow down a dirt path wide enough for four people to walk side by side. Ryann could see where Raz was taking him long before they got there. Up ahead about the length of a football field stood a giant tree dividing the horizon. The only thing he had to compare it to were the great redwood trees he had seen in books, only this one didn't appear to be quite that tall.

Daylight seemed to turn to dusk as they entered the shadow cast by the dense limbs and thick trunk. Ryann noted the trunk was so thick that a tunnel could be cut through it big enough for two cars to pass.

"This is the Tree of Life," Raz spoke proudly, as if sharing a grand secret. "It was given to us at the beginning of time by the Word."

Ryann noticed that his ring had started glowing white again, but ignored it to ask more about the tree. "What does it mean?"

"It's His promise to us of life together for all who eat its fruit."

Ryann peered closer into the thick branches at the oval-shaped fruit. He had never seen anything like it. About the same size as an avocado, the fruit was a warm pinkish-red color that appeared ripe for eating.

"Ahem!" A smooth, delicate voice from behind them interrupted his thoughts. Jerking around, Ryann instinctively froze as he stared into the face of a spotted leopard. The dangerous animal stood just twenty feet away, but with no cage between them. Ryann quickly glanced at Raz.

"Hello, Esselyt, I'd like to introduce a new friend of mine—Ryann."

"It's a pleasure to make your acquaintance," the leopard quipped.

Ryann remained motionless. He gazed into the creature's eyes and tried to speak, but no words came out.

"What's the matter? Cat got your tongue?" the leopard grinned.

"Give him a break, Essy. I'm sure he's never seen a talking leopard."

"Thanks, Raz," Ryann said, acknowledging his new friend. "But I can take care of myself."

"No harm meant," the leopard replied. "I couldn't help but notice your unusual clothing and items you were carrying, so I had to have a closer look."

Ryann looked the big cat over. Her coat was smooth and shiny, as if a gloss had been painted over the golden fur that was littered with brown spots. Esselyt, or Essy as Raz had called her, was indeed a beautiful creature. "Somehow the word *creature* no longer fits animals that can talk, but it will take a lot of getting used to," Ryann thought.

"So, where did you come from?" Essy asked.

Ryann quickly recounted the story of fishing at a small lake, the golden circle appearing, and jumping into it. "The next thing I knew, I was here."

"Jumping into a glowing circle in the water?" Essy said, "That seems either very brave or very foolish."

"My ring was glowing gold, and I just had this feeling that it was the right thing to do at the time," Ryann defended himself.

"This ring of yours—where did you get it?"

"From an angel. He gave it to me, as well as this staff and horn. He said that I was to seek the King's sword...that," Ryann searched for the right words, "that the Spirit would lead me and the ring would open the way."

"There's no doubt in my mind," Raz spoke up, "the Word has brought you here."

"I would have to agree. Everything points to it," Essy concurred with a nodding head.

Ryann looked back and forth between the two, but both of them were staring at his hand. The ring had returned to glowing white.

"I don't know what it means."

"The last time it was white, we were talking about the Word as well," Raz said. "Perhaps it has to do with conversations about Him?"

"Or, I wonder," said Essy, "how about this...the Word is not truthful."

Immediately, the shining white disappeared and was quickly replaced by the normal clear bubble.

"Wow! What'd you do?" Ryann asked.

"Just a minute," Essy snapped back, "and now...uh...let me think; guard your heart, for it is the wellspring of life."

Immediately the ring returned to the white glow from a few seconds ago.

"Mmm...I see...I see," Raz nodded.

"See what? What's going on?" Ryann asked, frustrated by the two animals seeming like know-it-alls.

"Well," began Raz, "it appears as if the white glow occurs when the truth is spoken. Am I correct, Essy?"

"Quite. You see, Ryann, when I said the Word is not truthful, the ring stopped glowing, but when I quoted something the Word has spoken to us, your ring instantly changed back to white. What you have is a way to determine if someone is saying the truth or not."

"Wow!" Ryann exclaimed. "It turns white for truth, blue when I'm around water, and so far it's turned gold for a way to get here. I wonder what other colors it changes to."

The fine, smooth fur above Essy's eyes scrunched up as she spoke, "And what, pray tell, do the other gifts bestowed upon you by the angel do? Shoot fire?"

"Actually," Ryann said, "I'm not sure; I've never given 'em a try. Why don't I give it a shot right now? Fire would be pretty cool."

"Cool?" Raz scrunched his brow.

"Never mind," Ryann said, thinking Raz sounded like his parents.

Ryann extended the smooth metal shaft with both hands. He wasn't quite sure what this thing would do, but he wanted it as far from his body as he could get it. Ryann warned, "You two might want to back away. No telling what might happen." Wincing, he lifted his thumb and slowly placed it over the first button. "OK...here goes," Ryann announced, his eyes almost shut.

Phhzzzzatt! Noise squelched the staff as a small stream of sparks flew out the end, followed by a puff of black smoke. "Whoa!" Ryann yelped, almost dropping the staff as he jerked his thumb off the button, waving his arms about wildly.

The raucous laughter filling the air was a surprise, and Ryann felt his ears burn. Turning his attention away from the staff, he glared at the leopard and raccoon, heads tilted back and mouths open, bellowing out of control.

"What…what's so funny?" Ryann snapped.

Raz quickly gained control, "Oh! So sorry, so sorry, I just couldn't help it…the way you were flailing about and…your eyes. They went from being almost closed to bulging out of your head!"

Essy was still whooping it up. "Get back! Get back! No telling what might happen!" The leopard howled, standing on her hind legs and sticking her paws out to imitate Ryann.

"All right, knock it off, fuzz face," Ryann challenged. "Better safe than sorry."

Essy looked over at Raz, who had his paws crossed in front of his chest, staring back. Dropping back down on all fours, Essy became serious again, "Why don't you try one of the other numbers, Ryann. I promise not to laugh this time."

Ryann held the staff out again, but this time he didn't squint as he pushed down the second button. Nothing. Then the third. Fourth. Fifth, sixth, seventh—still nothing.

"I can't imagine Gabriel giving me a staff lined with buttons that don't do anything to help in my search for the sword. There must be something else to it."

Raz agreed. "Like the ring, I suppose you'll have to figure it out."

Essy suggested, "How about your horn—why not give it a blow?"

Ryann laid the staff down and reached for the horn hanging off his hip. Pulling it forward, Ryann raised an eyebrow at his two new friends, "I'm not a professional trumpet player, so no laughing this time."

"Oh, wouldn't think of it!" Essy assured him. Ryann thought he saw a slim smile on her face.

"Here goes nothing," Ryann said, taking a deep gulp of air and puckering his lips. Ryann blew as hard and long as he could.

Buuuuwahhhhhhhhh!

He didn't want to appear weak or look bad in front of the two again. The deep moan broke through the air with the first half of Ryann's breath and then slowly rose to a harsh whine as his face grew red. Birds chirped and flew out of nearby trees as the unique note echoed all around them.

Ryann finally pulled the horn away from his lips after a full ten seconds. As his cheeks returned from beet red to their normal color, he turned to look in Raz and Essy's direction. Both stared wide-eyed straight ahead, as if looking past him.

"What, what's the matter?" Ryann asked.

Their mouths were both open, and they shivered like they had experienced a sudden chill.

"Come on you two, snap out of it," Ryann yelled.

They both turned their heads slowly to look at him, seemed to shake out of it, and then almost in unison said, "Let's go. We need to get out of here."

Ryann didn't know what was going on, but he was in unfamiliar territory, so he scrambled after the two four-footed creatures as they scurried through the tall grass back to the edge of the forest. Making their way just inside the tree line, Raz and Essy stopped.

"What's going on?" Ryann asked.

The two looked at each other as if wondering the same thing, shrugged their furry shoulders, and looked back at Ryann. Raz was the first to speak.

"I don't know what it was," he started. "One minute you were blowing your horn and the next it was as if something was wrong. I can't place exactly what it was, but it felt eerie, like something bad was about to happen."

"That's how I felt too, Raz," Essy added.

"Maybe it had something to do with the horn," Ryann said, "but let's leave it alone for now. I want to know more about Aeliana."

The three of them sat in a circle at the edge of the grassy plain, Raz giving a history lesson on their world, while Essy interrupted occasionally with the vivid details about a glorious winged Pegasus or fire-breathing dragon. Ryann found it fascinating and couldn't wait to see more of Aeliana, but as they came to the end of their story, he was reminded of what had brought him here.

"It's all so fascinating," Ryann acknowledged. "But, how am I supposed to locate the sword Gabriel told me to find?"

"That is a puzzle, isn't it?' Raz said. "Let's travel around Lake Penwyn while I think about it."

Ryann and Essy, who had no objections, fell in a few paces behind Raz.

"Raz is a pretty sharp fellow. I'd imagine by the time we get to the lake he'll have it all figured out," Essy said.

The scenery didn't change much as they walked the well-worn path, but Ryann knew they were getting close when his ring started glowing blue.

"It's just up ahead," Raz announced over his shoulder.

"Yeah, I know," Ryann answered, holding up his hand and pointing to it when Essy looked over. "I've got to have some answers. I need to know what to do next," Ryann said just loud enough for Essy to hear.

"He'll think of something."

Another twenty feet and they had caught up to Raz on the edge of a huge lake. The sun was setting behind them, casting a net of odd-shaped shadows across the clear water as golden-orange hues strained to get past the tree tops and hills. The only sound and ripples in the water were caused by the same falls they had looked down from earlier in the day. Raz sat on his haunches staring across the water.

Ryann waited a few moments before breaking the silence. "Well, what do you think I should do?"

Raz remained motionless, but answered, "I'm not so sure you should *do* anything."

"What do you mean not do anything? I have to do something. The angel said to search out and put on the full armor of God."

"There is a difference between doing and searching, Ryann. Searching requires not only looking on the outside, but also looking on the inside."

Essy interrupted. "Ryann! Your ring!"

All eyes focused on the gold tone radiating from Ryann's hand. The water just offshore began bubbling in a small circle that slowly began to expand and turn golden-tan.

"It would appear that this is your cue, my friend," Raz said.

"No!" Ryann pleaded. "It can't be. I'm not ready to go yet."

"It's OK, Ryann. His ways are not our ways. The Word must have a reason for calling you back to your world. Whatever it is, be willing to search more and do less."

"You're right, Raz. Thanks. I hope to see both of you again." For the second time that day, Ryann jumped into the glittery gold circle, this time watching his new friends as he disappeared beneath the surface. And then, for the second time that day, he found himself wondering what was going to greet him on the other side.

CHAPTER 5

Sea of Skepticism

RYANN WASN'T SURE where the golden pathway between Aeliana and his world would take him. His two concerns were that his parents would be distraught over him getting home so late and what had become of Terell and Drake. Terell, his best friend, had been left to defend himself against the class bully. Only now did Ryann truly realize what he had done—deserted a friend when he needed him most. He pictured Terell's troubled face as he jumped into the lake and knew he had to find him as soon as possible.

Just as before, Ryann felt his legs burst through the bubble first, then the rest of his body oozed through until his feet touched solid ground. He re-emerged into daylight and squinted his eyes to shield them from the sun. He wondered if it was the same day. Turning around, he realized he wasn't by the lake. He was in his own backyard!

Ryann's backyard was unique in his neighborhood because of the steeply sloped and wooded lot that covered almost an acre. He stood next to the clubhouse Liddy, Terell, and he had built a few years ago in the far corner of the yard. Made out of scrap wood and other garage throwaways, it was sturdier than it looked and was designed as a place to escape.

Ryann had to find out what time it was, whether Terell was OK, and where Gabriel's gifts were. His ring was still on his hand, but the staff and horn were gone. Ryann began the long trek up their steep, wooded yard. Chest heaving and out of breath, he opened the door, raced through the kitchen, and bounded up the narrow stairwell to his room.

"Ryann?" he heard his mom call out, "Is that you?"

"Yes, ma'am!'"

"I thought you were going fishing after school?"

"We did, Mom. I'm already back."

"Did you run out of bait? It's only four thirty." His mom continued to carry on the conversation by yelling instead of coming into his room.

Ryann didn't answer. "Four thirty?" he wondered. "It's only been thirty minutes since I left? I must have been in Aeliana for at least three and a half or four hours. How in the world could time have gone by so slow here and moved so much quicker there?"

He had only considered the idea for a moment when another thought barged in. The closet! He lunged to the closet door and slid it open. Moving his clothes aside, he found the staff and horn lying where he had originally hidden them. He was going to have to give this a lot more thought. He had no control over the angel's gifts. He couldn't carry them with him through the golden gateway to Aeliana or back, yet somehow they followed him.

A distant ring mingled with his thoughts about the time difference and the gifts moving.

His mother yelled from downstairs. "Ryann! It's for you!"

Ryann ran into his parent's room to answer the phone.

"Hello?"

"Yo, man, where did you go?" It was Terell.

"You're never going to believe it. I went to another world called Aeliana. I met a raccoon named Raz and his leopard friend, Esselyt, actually Essy for short and—"

"Whoa, whoa, whoa, slow down, dude. What do you mean another world?"

"That gold stuff I jumped into—it was some sort of tunnel to another world. Let's meet at the clubhouse in ten minutes and I'll tell you all about it."

Retelling the story could have been done in twenty minutes, but with Terell continually interrupting to get more details, it took about an hour.

"And then I came back through the golden tunnel and ended up right outside the old clubhouse," Ryann concluded.

"Whoa, that's wild, man," Terell shook his head.

"Oh, my gosh!" Ryann said. "What happened between you and Drake?"

"Mmm…I thought I was in for a mess of trouble, but when Drake saw you jump in, he freaked and took off running in the other direction."

"I'm sorry for taking off like that, Terell," Ryann said softly, shaking his head. "I really didn't mean to leave you alone. Will you forgive me?"

"Dude, you're my best friend. Of course I'll give it up for you. By the way, man, your bike is over at my house. I had to call my mom to come and get me. With you out of the picture and the way Drake dented the frames when he knocked them over, there was no other way to get both of them home."

"Thanks, man," Ryann said as they rapped knuckles.

"So what happens now, Ryann?"

"Both Raz and Essy were convinced that the sword would be found in Aeliana."

"Why?"

"They figured since Gabriel gave me the ring, and the ring alerted me to the golden tunnel, that it was his way of directing me. Gabriel himself told me the ring would open the way."

"But you didn't find it while you were there, and the ring brought you back again."

"Yeah, I've got a feeling that this isn't going to be easy," Ryann said.

"So," Terell wrung his hands together, "that brings me back to my original question. What happens now?"

"I start studying."

"Studying?"

"Remember what I said Gabriel's last words were to me? He said, 'All Scripture is God-breathed and is useful for teaching.' I'm gonna take him up on it and get out my Bible."

"That's cool. Let me know if you find anything."

"You'll be the first."

"You gonna tell Liddy?"

"Yeah, I'll call her tonight. She's part of the group."

Terell turned, looked through the secret spy hole to see if anyone was directly outside. "All clear," he announced, opening the door. "See ya tomorrow, Ryann."

"Yeah, see ya." Ryann leaned back in his chair, hands behind his head, as his mind drifted off to Aeliana.

Ryann's family almost always ate dinner together, and tonight was no exception. They sat, in order by age, around a round table. It was the only one Ryann could ever remember sitting at. He shoveled his food down as fast as he could, grimacing a little with each mouthful of peas. Ryann knew he could only go so fast. There was an unwritten family rule that you had to sit at the table for a certain period of time before you could ask to be excused. His parents had never said how long it was, but Ryann figured it was about fifteen minutes.

"May I be excused, please?" Ryann asked his father at what he perceived to be the appropriate time.

"That was quick," his father said. Ryann watched his father glance at his mother and then at his plate to see if his food was gone. "Sure, Ryann, do you have something important to get to?"

"Oh, you know, homework."

"You seem awfully eager to get started," his mother said, looking up from her plate. "Uh, yes, ma'am. I have a special project to work on."

Ryann's mother and father made eye contact again. "You're excused," his father said. "Let us know if we can be of any help."

Ryann took his plate to the sink, rinsed it off, and put it in the dishwasher. It was a routine at the Watters's household that started at six years of age. Stepping lightly over to the stairwell, Ryann fought his impulse to race up the stairs. His parents hadn't let him have a phone in his room, so he made his way into their room before anyone else left the dinner table.

"Hello, Mrs. Thomas, this is Ryann. May I speak with Liddy, please?" The receiver shook in his hand.

"Sure, Ryann, let me get her for you," Mrs. Thomas said.

He couldn't wait to share the news with Liddy. She hadn't been able to share the excitement of his jumping into the golden circle, but he knew she'd enjoy hearing about everything that had happened.

"Hey, Ryann, what's up?" Liddy asked.

"Liddy, you're not going to believe this, but today I visited another world."

There was no response.

"Liddy? Are you there?"

"I'm here," she answered in a monotone voice.

"Well, anyway, it was amazing, I met a talking raccoon and leopard and—"

"You're right, Ryann."

"What do you mean?"

"You're right, I don't believe you."

It took Ryann a moment to realize what Liddy had said. She didn't believe him! How could she not think he was telling the truth? Ryann was hurt, but then his face scrunched into a scowl and he fought to keep his voice low. "What do you mean you don't believe me?"

"Come on, Ryann, do you really expect me to believe you've been to another world?"

"But I have, Liddy. What about the ring? You saw it glowing," Ryann pleaded his case.

"Yeah, I'm beginning to have my doubts about that, too," she said. "Are you sure this isn't something Terell and you thought up?"

"No, Liddy, honest," Ryann said.

"Mmm, well, I'm going to have to see it myself to believe it. Hey, sorry, gotta go." Click.

Ryann slowly lowered the phone to the receiver. A knot formed in his stomach, making him want to double over, like he had just been punched. Dragging his feet across the thick carpet, he staggered down the hall to his room and closed the door gently behind him. Dropping into his desk chair, Ryann slouched down and fixed his gaze on the darkness outside his bedroom window. He couldn't understand why Liddy didn't believe him.

"Ryann! Telephone!" his mom yelled up the stairs.

Ryann jerked in his chair. Maybe it was Liddy calling to apologize. Racing back down the hall to his parent's room, Ryann grabbed the phone again. "Hello?"

"Yo, Ryann, it's me," Terell said. "Have you figured anything out yet?"

"No."

"Nothing at all?"

"No," he answered again blankly.

"What's wrong, dude? You sound upset."

"It's Liddy," Ryann said. "I called her to tell her what happened and she doesn't believe me. She thinks I'm making it up."

"Don't let her get you down, man. Just keep working on figuring out what's going on. We'll prove it to her," Terell encouraged.

"Yeah, I guess you're right. Thanks, Terell."

"No problem. Now get your Bible off the shelf and see if you can find any clues to what's going on. I'll meet you tomorrow after school at the Sweet Shoppe. That should give us some time away from everyone, and you can fill me in."

Ryann grabbed his Bible off the bookshelf and thought about how great it was to have a trusted friend like Terell. Spurred on by the encouragement, Ryann opened his Bible to the center—Proverbs. "Mmm, didn't Solomon write that?" Ryann thought, "The wisest man ever? Maybe I should start looking for clues here." Not knowing what he should be looking for, Ryann tried to recall what Essy had quoted from the Word when his ring glowed white for truth. "Something about guarding your heart," he remembered. Flipping to the concordance in back, he carefully trailed his index finger down the page: Grumble… Guarantee…Guard. There it was, Proverbs 4:23. He quickly turned back to Proverbs and found the verse, "Above all else, guard your heart, for it is the wellspring of life."

"Wellspring of life? What does that mean?" he wondered. Ryann knew he needed to protect his heart. There were all sorts of notes at the bottom of the page relating to the verses above. Ryann found 4:23: "If we store up good things in our hearts, our words and actions will be good."

"It's like a puzzle," Ryann noted—find the key words in back, read the verse, find out more about the meaning below, and then it lists another verse to check."

Ryann quickly turned back a page to the second chapter of Proverbs. Scanning down the page he let out a loud, "Yes!" He glanced at his door and paused in case any of his family had heard him and come in. After a few minutes he turned his attention back to his Bible, anxiously drawing lines over the first few verses with a yellow highlighter. "If you accept my words and store up my commands within you, turning your ear to wisdom and applying your heart to understanding, and if you call out for insight and cry aloud for understanding, and if you look for it as for silver and search for it as for hidden treasure, then you will understand the fear of the LORD and find the knowledge of God."

"There are a lot of *ifs*. I've accepted His words, so now I need to 'store up commands,'" Ryann considered. "That must mean learn more about what God says in the Bible," he thought. "'Turning your ear'? Mmm...down below here it says, 'Listening means obedience.' I'm obeying by searching for the sword. 'If you call out for understanding'— I haven't done that yet. Maybe I should ask God for help. Then I need to search for it like silver and hidden treasure. Both of those are in the ground; maybe that's a clue. If I do all that, I'll understand the fear of the Lord and find the knowledge of God. Wow! This is going to be a lot of work," Ryann reasoned.

He yawned, looked down at the notes he had scribbled, then over to his digital alarm clock to see what time it was. "Ten thirty, already? No wonder I'm so tired," he sighed. After standing and stretching, he slid open his closet door to check on his staff and horn. His clothes hung so tightly together, they formed a thick wall, so Ryann had decided hanging his staff and horn behind them would keep them better hidden. Removing a small section of clothes, Ryann leaned in to reach the back of the closet until he felt the familiar smooth metal staff. Pulling it out, he was about to reach back for the horn, when he noticed the buttons on the staff—the first one was lit!

Ryann backed up, stumbling on his chair. "What does it mean? Should I call Terell? No, it's too late. I'll have to wait until I see him tomorrow," he thought. He ran his fingers over the button, first the lit one and then the other six. They felt the same, but Ryann knew that something was different. Things had changed since he came back from Aeliana, but he wasn't sure just what. Reflecting on the day, there was a lot to learn; a new world, Raz and Essy, Liddy not believing him, and now a button on his staff lighting up. At least Terell believed him, and maybe tomorrow they'd find some more answers together.

Chapter 6

Betrayed

RAKE SAT ALONE in his room, running his hands across the smooth, black cloak given to him by Lord Ekron. Following Terell and Ryann after school to the lake had been a hunch on his part. Their faces had flushed with guilt when he approached Liddy and them in class to ask what they were talking about. Lord Ekron had told him that he needed to stop the one who seeks to bind, and the first two likely candidates were Terell and Ryann. The decision to corner the two of them out by the lake and intimidate them was easy. What he hadn't expected was the strange glowing water and Ryann's disappearance. Even now he could see the blank, distant stare from Ryann's eyes as he slipped beneath the surface. Panicking, he had run as quickly as he could back to his bicycle and raced the entire way home.

"I blew it," Drake thought. "It was my first chance to do something for Lord Ekron and I chickened out." Drake smashed his fist down on his desk, hoping for another chance.

"Things not going as well as you would have liked?" the crackling voice muttered from behind him.

He jumped slightly. "Oh," he said, turning to see his aunt standing in the doorway, the small lamp in his room casting eerie shadows across her face. "You startled me."

She smiled when he said that, as she crossed the room and placed her long, bony fingers on his shoulder. "Do you feel like you let him down?" she asked.

"Let him down?" he wondered. "She couldn't be talking about Lord Ekron, could she? How could she know?"

"What do you mean?" Drake asked his aunt. "Let who down?"

"It's okay, boy, it's not a secret. Lord Ekron first visited me many years ago when I was a girl about your age. I've done his bidding ever since. He's the one who told me to adopt you."

Drake glared at her, caught between the desire for her to tell him more about Lord Ekron and despising her for revealing the harsh truth that he wasn't adopted because of family loyalty, but out of obligation.

"If you're like me, you can feel the power that he has to offer. Then you won't have to worry about anyone taking advantage of you again," she said.

Drake stared into the empty, sagging eyes that glared back at him. Ever since he could remember, he had felt uncomfortable around his aunt. She always seemed to be staring at him, like she was peering into his thoughts. He didn't think she really could, but Drake always felt she knew more than she was letting on.

"I'm afraid I've outlived my usefulness, but he has plans for you, Drake. I see you have his symbol." She stared at the red dragon on the black ring. "Now that you've opened the door and let him in, there can be no turning back."

Drake considered her words. "Why would I want to turn back? Lord Ekron is opening my eyes to things I've never seen before," he reasoned. Suddenly his aunt didn't seem so scary anymore. She looked tired and frail.

"Do you know who Lord Ekron wants you to stop?"

He hesitated and then look deep into her eyes. "I have an idea."

"Then you must attack his weakness. Does he have any friends?"

"Yes, his best friend is in our class at school."

"Tell me his name," she said, closing her eyes.

"Uh, Terell…Terell Peterson," Drake answered, watching his aunt closely as she began mumbling to herself. Then she stopped muttering and seemed to quit breathing all together. Drake jumped when her eyes suddenly opened wide, glaring through him as if he wasn't there.

"Terell Peterson will be at The Sweet Shoppe tomorrow at three-thirty. You must get there before Ryann and ask him about the sword and the Word," her voice trailing off into a whisper.

Drake watched in amazement as the old woman's eyes shut again, her head flopped down, and shoulders slumped. Jumping out of his seat, he reached out to steady her frail body in case she fell. Her skin felt like a wet baseball glove. Gripping his arm, Aunt Belial perked up, refreshed. She peered into his eyes. "There are a few more things you need to know," she said firmly, increasing the pressure on his arm as she continued whispering hoarsely in his ear. At the point when he was ready to cry out, she finished, abruptly releasing her grip, and turned away, shuffling out of the room.

Terell paced back and forth just outside The Sweet Shoppe, sat down in one of the sidewalk chairs, rocked back and forth a few times, then stood up and began pacing again. He was twenty minutes early and read the familiar sign for the millionth time, Thomas Sweet Homemade Ice Cream and Fudge. He told Ryann to be here after school at three thirty, and everyone knew Ryann was always on time. Stepping up to the outdoor counter, he ordered a single scoop of his favorite flavor, butter pecan. Just as he was about to take his first lick, a voice boomed out behind him.

"Hey, Terell, how ya doing?"

Terell's stomach sank. There was no mistaking Drake's voice, and nothing good ever came from being around him. Turning to face him, Terell managed a weak smile.

"H-H-Hi, Drake, what a surprise seeing ya...you here. A-are you looking for someone?"

"I'm looking for someone who knows something about another world. You wouldn't happen to know someone like that would you?"

"Uh, no," Terell said.

"Mmm, that's funny," Drake said, taking a step closer and lowering his voice. "I thought you might know something about a sword."

"I, I, da...da...don't know anything about a sword, Drake," Terell said, inching backwards, the ice cream in his cone dripping over the sides and down his fingers.

Drake pressed forward until Terell felt the rough bricks behind him and Drake's heavy breathing on his face.

"I know you know about these things, Terell. Now tell me about *the Word*!"

"I, I swear Drake, I've ne...never heard of any of this before!"

The loud screech overhead startled them both. A hawk circled high above; floating in a deep, blue sky. Drake was only diverted for a moment.

"I think you're lying, Terell, and before Ryann gets here I want to know everything you know."

Terell looked to his right and left. There was nowhere to go and he was physically no match for Drake. Terell stole a peek at his watch. Ryann wouldn't be there for another ten minutes. He focused his eyes on the sidewalk and dropped the melting ice cream into the trashcan next to him.

"Wa...what do you want to know?"

Ryann whistled as he strode down Fifth Avenue toward Terell and his favorite meeting spot, The Sweet Shoppe. Actually, Dickens-Reed Book Nook was where they met the most, to play chess on one of the small tables in the café area and check on the latest books. The Nook, as they called it, was unique because it not only had new and used books, but also specialized in books on Florida and had a special section just for kids. But they loved to meet at The Sweet Shoppe so they could get ice cream.

As he made his way across the street expecting to see an excited Terell waiting for him, a screech pierced the air from high overhead. Ryann watched the reddish-brown bird float on the air, while trying to recall if he had ever seen a bird like that in Mount Dora. He couldn't wait to tell Terell about his new findings, snapping his fingers to confirm his good mood as he hopped up onto the sidewalk. Terell wasn't in front of the store, and a quick glance up and down the street didn't reveal his friend, either.

"I'm afraid Terell won't be joining you," said Drake as he stepped out from an alcove in the storefront.

"What do you mean, Drake?" Ryann took a step backward.

"It seems your friend had other plans, that is, after he told me everything he knows," Drake sneered.

Ryann clenched his fists. He knew he wasn't a match for Drake physically. But he couldn't stand by and let his friend be pushed around by a bully.

"Why don't you pick on someone your own size, Drake? Like someone over at the high school."

Drake laughed, "Yeah…he told me all about the sword you're trying to find, the angel who visited you, and what was it? Oh, yeah, the staff and horn you have?"

Ryann's shoulders slumped as he look questioningly at Drake.

"Sometimes we think we know who our friends are," said Drake, as if reading Ryann's mind. "And then they go and do something like this."

"What'd you do to him, Drake? Where is he now?"

Drake stepped forward until his face was inches away from Ryann's. Lowering his voice to a hoarse whisper, Drake answered, "I wouldn't worry about your friend. I'd be more worried about yourself."

Ryann was pretty sure Drake wouldn't do anything to him in such a public place. He tried matching Drake's glare by staring back into his eyes. Something didn't seem right, and Ryann quickly looked away. Were his eyes deceiving him, or had Drake's eyes flashed between his normal green to red, and back again?

Ryann turned and started sprinting as fast as he could. He didn't need to look back to see if he was being followed. Drake's voice could be heard far behind bellowing, "You can run, but you can't hide, Ryann…I'm going to be watching you!"

Ryann retreated back the way he had come, then turned up McDonald Street toward his church. Shaking his head in disbelief, he slowed to a walk.

How could Terell tell Drake about everything? Ryann grimaced as he kicked at a rock on the sidewalk. "And Liddy…she doesn't even believe anything I say any more," he recalled.

"It's hopeless…I wish Gabriel had never come and everything would just be back the way it was," he decided to himself.

Ryann's eyes drifted up as he approached the back of "First Prez," as everyone called it. Someone was lying on the bench. He was sure it was Noah.

Ryann stood beside the sleeping man and looked down at him. He still wore the same tattered suit he had the first time Ryann saw him. Despite the man's wrinkly-tan face and crumpled clothes, Ryann couldn't help but think there was something different about him. He seemed so at peace.

"Life is full of twists and turns, isn't it?" the man asked without opening his eyes.

"Ahh!" gasped Ryann, jumping back.

A sly, white grin spread across Noah's face. Then his eyes opened.

"Geez, Noah! You scared me to death."

The old man laughed as he pushed himself up to a sitting position. "You shouldn't be sneaking up on a man my age. So...how's life treating you?"

Ryann glanced down at his shoes.

"That bad, huh? Do you want to talk about it?"

"I just don't know what to do," Ryann took a deep breath. "I've been betrayed by my best friend. Another good friend doesn't think I'm telling her the truth. And, to top all of that, there's a bully who wants to beat me up."

Noah whistled."That does seem to be a lot for one young man to handle. So...is there anyone who can help you out of this mess?"

"I was thinking about asking my parents for help, but I haven't told them about..." Ryann caught himself, "I mean they don't know everything that's going on right now."

"Your parents would probably be a good place to start. They have your best interests at heart. Although..." Noah paused and lowered his voice, "there's someone else who cares about you even more."

Ryann peered into the weatherworn face and couldn't help but center his attention on the bright blue eyes sparkling back at him. He could sense there was something different about this old hobo.

"Who could care about me more than my parents? Are you talking about God?" Ryann asked.

"I am," Noah answered with a kind smile. "He loves you because you are His creation."

"Then why is He letting all of these bad things happen to me?"

"Oh…adults ask themselves and others that question all the time. Have you ever heard them ask how a loving God could allow them to lose their job or not have things go the way they had planned for their life?"

Ryann nodded.

Noah continued, "They don't stop to think that because God loves them so much He doesn't allow things to go as they plan. Like your father, our heavenly Father knows what is best for us."

"But," Ryann hesitated, trying to find the right words, "how can what I'm going through possibly be good for me?"

"Do you have faith?"

"Faith?"

"Do you believe that God really loves you and has a special plan for your life?"

Ryann pondered the old man's words. "I…I think I do."

"Thinking in your head and believing in your heart are two different things, Ryann." Noah motioned for Ryann to come and sit next to him. Once there, the old man put his arm around Ryann's shoulder.

His touch seemed firm and reassuring instead of frail, like Ryann had expected.

Noah continued, "A friend of mine, James, said that you should be happy when you face tough times, because it tests your faith. And, testing of your faith develops perseverance."

"Why would I want to develop perseverance?"

"He answered that, too," Noah said, "because when you finish persevering you will be mature, complete, and receive the crown of life."

"First a sword and now a crown? This is beginning to be too much," Ryann said, glancing down at his watch. "I've gotta go."

"Don't forget our talk, Ryann," Noah said as the boy stood up and half scampered away. "It will come back to help you!"

"Thanks, Noah! I'm feeling better already," he yelled back over his shoulder.

Return to Aeliana

"**H**OMEWORK AGAIN, RYANN?" asked his father when Ryann asked to be excused from dinner that night.

"No, sir, not on a Friday night; it's a special project." Ryann had hoped not to appear suspicious, but he had to get up to his room and see what else he could find out from the Bible.

"Okay, son, you're excused." Ryann scooted out of his seat and strode as casually as he could over to the sink to wash his plate off. "And Ryann?" his father added, "Good job, not waiting until the last minute to start a project for school."

"Thanks," Ryann replied as he slipped around the corner and leapt up the stairs, two at a time, to his bedroom.

Opening his notebook, Ryann wrote the date at the top of a new page. He had decided to keep notes of everything that was happening, just in case he needed it later, to find a clue. Now what was it Noah had said?

Ryann opened his Bible to the Table of Contents and began running his finger down the list. From Sunday school class, he knew the Bible was made up of sixty-six books, thirty-nine in the Old Testament and twenty-seven in the New Testament. His finger rested on one that stood out among the rest—James. Hadn't Noah said he had a friend named James? "It couldn't be the same guy—" Ryann thought, "this book would have been written almost two thousand years ago." He decided to try it anyway and opened up to the book of James.

"Here it is," Ryann whispered to himself. His eyes had quickly glanced past the introduction to the second verse. It was the same thing Noah had said: "Consider it pure joy, my brothers, whenever you face trials of many kinds, because you know that the testing of your faith develops perseverance. Perseverance must finish its work so that you may be mature and complete, not lacking anything."

Ryann wondered what he was supposed to do now. He continued reading to see if he would find an answer. "If any of you lacks wisdom, he should ask God, who gives generously to all without finding fault, and it will be given to him." Ryann scribbled it down in his journal and underlined it. "God…gives generously to all without finding fault, but…" Ryann circled the word *but*. He knew from his parents that what followed was something he was going to have to do. Scrawling again, he copied the rest, "But when he asks, he must believe and not doubt, because he who doubts is like a wave of the sea, blown and tossed by the wind."

Ryann stared at the words he had written, mulling over each one. He figured he certainly must be getting tested right now, and the solution seemed to be to ask God for wisdom. Ryann had prayed with his family before meals and most of the time before he went to bed, but he had never really prayed on his own.

He hoped his request wouldn't be based on "style points." Closing his eyes, Ryann bowed his head and began uttering in short spurts, "Uh...God? It's me, Ryann. I know the words say to ask You, for uhh...wisdom, so...as You can see, I'm in need of it. Please give me some, so I know what to do." Ryann opened one eye just enough to sneak a peek at the verse. He didn't want to forget the part about not doubting. "Oh, and God...I believe that You really are going to answer me."

"Now what?" Ryann thought, glancing about the room. His focus came to rest on the folding closet door that was partially open. An odd glow was seeping out from behind his clothes. "My staff!" Ryann snapped, leaping out of his seat and pushing the clothes apart. The staff stood upright, just as he had left it, only now two of the buttons were lit. Ryann reached out tentatively to grab it, half expecting to be shocked in the process. He winced when he first touched the smooth metal surface, then relaxed. He thought about all of the things that might happen if he pushed one of the buttons. Maybe fire? Or, perhaps a lightening bolt? Who knows, but he wasn't foolish enough to try it inside. Ryann laughed to himself as he pictured his parents bursting into a smoke-filled room with a large hole blown in the side of his bedroom wall.

He had to share the good news with someone, but whom? Terell had betrayed him, and Liddy didn't believe him. "Maybe I should just call them both and try to get us all together and review where we are now," he thought.

The first call to Terell ended up with Ryann in a short conversation with Mrs. Peterson. Terell was sick in bed and was hoping he would make it to church on Sunday. The call to Liddy was more successful. She at least agreed to hear "all the evidence," as she put it. They would meet over at her house after lunch. Ryann felt better when he got off the phone. He was determined to make Liddy believe.

Lake Dora was a splendid backdrop for a clear, blue-sky afternoon. The water sparkled magically as Ryann cruised along Lakeshore Drive on his quickly aging bicycle. Drake had managed to put a few extra scratches and dings in it when he snuck up on Terell and Ryann at the fishing hole. As he approached Oakland Lane, Ryann turned sharply to his left and coasted down the paved embankment and under an old wooden truss that supported the Florida Central Rail Line.

Liddy's house was one of only two houses on the little stretch of land between the tracks and the lake. Ryann shot across the driveway through a small patch of grass to a majestic, hundred-year-old oak tree. He leaned his bike against the tree and trotted up the stone path to a castle-sized, dark wooden door. Ryann lifted the huge antique knocker and let it fall with a loud bang. While he waited for Liddy, he looked back and forth admiring the old European style house. Varying sizes of brown and gray stones outlined the windows and doors. Two dormers highlighted the roofline, and the moss hanging from the sprawling oak limbs gave the house a distinguished look that you would expect to see on a Hollywood movie set. Ryann wondered what it would be like to live on the lake as Liddy opened the door.

"How ya doing, Ryann?" Liddy asked good-naturedly, while not backing up to invite him in.

"Just great…uh, how about we talk out back so no one overhears us?" Ryann asked.

"No problem," Liddy said, brushing past him and heading toward the giant oak out back.

Ryann stepped along behind her, wondering how to get things started. He didn't have to worry as Liddy jumped right into business.

"So, Ryann, do you have some sort of proof to substantiate your wild tales about your trip to…what did you say that place was?"

"Aeliana."

"Right, Aeliana."

"I don't know if I can prove it to you exactly, Liddy. I have the ring," he said, whisking his hand in front of her face.

"I don't see how that proves anything," Liddy retorted. "I could probably buy a ring that lights up. Until I actually experience Aeliana for myself—I mean see it, touch it, smell it, really experience it—I'm not going to believe it."

They plopped down onto the bench beneath the lone, sprawling oak tree facing the water. Ryann gazed across the lake, trying to think of some sort of answer for Liddy. He wasn't sure if there was anything he could do to prove it to her.

"Is this another one of your jokes, Ryann?"

"Huh? What?" he asked, snapping out of his trance. "The other day your ring was glowing white, now it's pitch black."

Ryann glanced down at his hand in amazement. The stone was indeed black, a shiny reflective black. "I've never seen it that color before," he said. Something didn't seem right. Ryann glanced over his shoulder. A shadow at the corner of the house seemed to move.

"Come on, Liddy," Ryann said, jumping up. "Let's walk out to the dock."

Liddy scampered to catch up. "What's going on Ryann?" she demanded.

Ryann kept walking toward the dock. Holding his hand up and out in front of him, as if it were guiding him, Ryann watched in amazement as the stone flickered between black and blue.

"Come on, Ryann," Liddy insisted. "What's up?"

Ryann stopped at the edge of the recently refurbished dock. "It always turns blue when I'm near water. But it's never turned black before. I have no idea what that means."

Liddy didn't have a chance to respond before the ring changed colors again, this time to gold. "Now what?" she asked, intrigued.

Ryann didn't answer. Instead he treaded softly out onto the dock, gazing into the water, from one side to the other.

Liddy shadowed him, "What are you looking for?"

The ring turned black, then blue, then gold again. "There!" Ryann shouted, pointing off to the right, out in front of them.

Liddy peered into the water in amazement as the normally crystal blue water began turning gold. It grew in a matter of seconds from a small spot into a large circle. Then, as before, it began to bubble like boiling water on a stove, then sparkling brilliantly inches above the waterline.

"Hey! Whatcha guys doin'?"

Both Liddy and Ryann inhaled sharply as they whirled around to see Drake, arms crossed, his head cocked back and a sneer across his face.

Ryann stole a glance at his ring—black—then back to Drake.

Liddy spoke up first. "Drake, you weren't invited, so you can just leave now."

"Hey, Miss Smarty-pants, maybe I'm inviting myself. Something weird is going on out here, and I intend to find out what it is." Drake dropped his arms and stomped off across the yard toward them.

"Liddy," Ryann whispered without moving his lips.

"Yeah."

"Will you trust me?"

In a split second, Liddy's eyes darted from Ryann, to Drake, and down to the ring. It was flickering between black and gold. Without enough time to work through her usual analysis of a situation, Liddy went with her intuition, "Yes, I trust you."

As Drake approached the dock, Ryann grabbed Liddy's hand. "Jump!" he yelled, yanking hard on her arm and pulling her off the dock. Liddy's high-pitched scream filled the air as the two of them plunged into the bubbling gold water.

For Ryann, this second trip was much more enjoyable than the first. The pathway to Aeliana was familiar to him, and he remained almost motionless as they drifted down. Liddy on the other hand pulled her hand away from Ryann and flailed about trying to head for the surface and air. Ryann grabbed her arm, and when she turned to look at him, he just smiled.

It took a moment to register in her brain that they were both glowing under the water and that she could see Ryann as if they were still back on the dock. She couldn't feel the cold lake water, and instead of being able to swim up, she was gliding down. She had been in this lake hundreds of times and was an excellent swimmer. It didn't make sense. Looking over at Ryann again, he gave her the "thumbs up" sign, and even though his mouth didn't move, she heard him say, "You're safe, don't worry."

They had been underwater for more than a minute now, and she didn't have the panicky feeling that she needed to get up for air anymore. She knew he couldn't possibly hear her, but asked the question anyway, "Where are we?" She hadn't heard herself, but Ryann smiled and answered, "On our way to Aeliana." Liddy didn't see his mouth move, but she heard him just the same. Or had she imagined it? "Ryann? Can you hear me?" she asked.

Ryann smiled again and nodded. "Loud and clear."

"What happens next?"

"We'll float down until our feet touch something that feels like Jell-O, then we'll break through into Aeliana," Ryann answered.

Ryann was glad he could share the moment with someone. Until now, Terell and Liddy had to take his word for everything he said. Now, she'd have to believe. She had said it herself, "Until I actually experience Aeliana for myself—I mean see it, touch it, smell it, really experience it—I'm not going to believe it." Ryann knew that like himself, Liddy was about to have the experience of her life.

After they broke through, Ryann watched the glow on Liddy's face as she went through the same expressions he did on his first visit. He watched her take deep breaths, smelling the flowery aroma. Her blue eyes sparkled as she took in the vivid colors of Aeliana.

Back in Mount Dora, Drake had rushed out onto the dock in time to see Liddy and Ryann splash into the lake. It was the same gold-colored water he had seen Ryann jump into at Lake Franklin. Drake hesitated, wondering what to do next. As he stared at the gold circle below him, it began to shrink.

"Do not fail me again. Jump in now!" Drake heard the voice say.

Drake looked around. It sounded like Lord Ekron, but he didn't see anyone. "If they can do it, so can I," he thought. Gritting his teeth, Drake jumped off the dock, landing in the middle of the tightening gold circle. "They won't get away from me again," he promised himself, as he began the descent through the golden tunnel.

CHAPTER 8

ᴼᴶempest
ᴼᴶricks

Lᴵᴅᴅʏ ᴀʙsᴏʀʙᴇᴅ ᴇᴠᴇʀʏᴛʜɪɴɢ around her—the wavy grass, vibrant colors, and tingly smells. Her face beamed as she whirled around to Ryann and blurted out, "It's all so beautiful, Ryann, can you believe it?" As soon as she said it, she felt guilty. "Ryann I'm so sorry. I'm so sorry I didn't believe you."

Ryann smiled sheepishly. It wasn't often that Liddy had to admit she was wrong. "That's okay," he said, "I should actually be apologizing to you for pulling you in."

"Oh, no, I wouldn't want to miss this for anything. As long as you can get us back, of course."

"Can you help me look around?" Ryann asked. "I had a few things follow me the last time I was here." Leaning over, he sifted through the wild grass looking for his horn and staff. "I'm sure they're close by."

"Is this one?" Liddy held up his familiar staff. Ryann could see that the top two buttons were still lit. Liddy felt around where she had picked up the staff and quickly found the horn as well.

"Where did you get these, Ryann?"

"Gabriel gave them to me at the same time he gave me the ring." Taking the staff from Liddy, Ryann examined it closely, paying particular attention to the buttons. "You know," he said, "when Gabriel first gave this to me none of the buttons were lit up."

"How did they light up?" Liddy asked.

"I'm not exactly sure."

"What do you think would happen if you pushed one?"

"I tried last time I was here and nothing happened. But back then the buttons weren't lit," Ryann explained.

"Why don't you give it another try?" Liddy encouraged.

"All right, but stand back," Ryann said, holding the staff as far away from himself as he could. He looked at the way he was standing and quickly added, "And no laughing if nothing happens!" Ryann moved his thumb along the smooth surface until it rested on button number one. Ryann's arm tensed as he slowly squeezed the bony knob.

Phsssssssssst...a rainy mist shot out of the end of the staff, creating a thick cloud in front of them. Ryann could barely see through it. He waved the staff around and the cloud grew bigger and bigger. They both watched, amazed. Ryann didn't know what else to do, so he lifted his thumb, and the mist stopped shooting out of the staff, but the cloud remained for several minutes before it dissipated.

"Wow!" Liddy exclaimed. "That was awesome."

Ryann made sure to keep his fingers off the buttons and turned the staff over to see where the mist had come from. He hadn't noticed an opening before.

"Careful Ryann, that's like looking into the barrel of a gun," Liddy cautioned.

Ryann kept looking at the staff like he hadn't heard her. "Mmm...I wonder what the second button does?"

"Now's as good a time as any," encouraged Liddy.

"Stand back!"

More confident the second time around, Ryann squeezed slowly on button number two.

Whooooooosh.

Ryann cowered as fire spit out of the staff, forming a wall in front of him. His face awash in searing heat, Ryann tried to stare through the flames. But now it was a six-foot square wall of fire, and he couldn't see through it. Moving the staff from left to right, the wall passed in front of him. Raising the staff and his arms caused the wall of fire to leap up off the ground and maintain its shape in the air in front of him. "It's like having my own shield of fire," Ryann thought. Letting his thumb off the button, Liddy and he held their breath as the flames dissipated into a veil of smoke.

"That's amazing," Liddy whispered.

"That it is," Ryann agreed. "I'm just wondering what made them light up and why the others aren't."

"When was the first time they lit up?" Liddy asked.

"A few days ago the first one lit up, and then just last night the second one came on."

"Where were you when it happened? Your ring seems to change color based upon where you are."

"Mmm," Ryann hummed, then began talking softly to himself, "I was in my bedroom the first time…sitting at my desk…reading the Bible…and then the second time…" his whispering trailed off. "That's it!" Ryann yelped, startling Liddy as she raised a skeptical eyebrow.

"What's it, Ryann?"

"The buttons on the staff. They lit up separately, but each time one of them lit up, it was when I finished reading the Bible and learned something new about the quest."

"Interesting," Liddy nodded quizzically. "So you're saying that the more you learn, the more buttons will light up? We could have a problem." She grinned.

"Hey, watch it, Lydia."

They both laughed at Ryann's expense until Liddy's face became serious again. "Ryann, do you even know where we are in this place? What did you call it again?"

"No clue," he said flippantly. "As a matter of fact, we could have dropped into a different world for all I know." Ryann stayed serious as her eyes grew big. He couldn't hold it very long, and before she could reply his pursed lips broke into a giant smile. "Gotcha!" he laughed, pointing at her.

"Ryann Watters!" she yelled, realizing she was now on the receiving end of a brief prank. Folding her arms, Liddy gave him her "OK, now what?" look. "Well?" she asked.

"We're in Aeliana, pronounced El-ih-ah-nuh," Ryann answered, "and I think we aren't too far off from where I came through the first time." Stopping, he cocked his head, "If I'm not mistaken, that low rushing water sound is Glenys Falls, off to the East. And just beyond that is castle Myraddin."

Liddy listened intently, then acknowledged, "I guess I'm just going to have to trust you."

"Better late than never. Noah believes me, just from what I've told him."

"Who's Noah?"

"Haven't you ever seen him? He's that guy who's always on the park bench behind the church."

"You mean the bum?"

"He's not a bum, Liddy, he's a very wise old man. He's helped me think through some of the problems I've encountered with this whole quest. You know, you shouldn't judge people so quickly."

"Sorry, I guess I have a few shortcomings to work on." Liddy glanced down at her shoes.

"Hey, we've all got stuff to work on," Ryann answered her.

"So...what do we do next?" Liddy asked.

"In Aeliana, you never know how much time you have, so we'd better head off toward the castle. Hopefully we'll run into Raz and Essy along the way." Ryann gripped his staff firmly and handed the horn to Liddy. "Here, why don't you carry this?

I'm not sure exactly what it does yet, but that way we'll be able to use it and the staff in case we need them at the same time."

Liddy slipped her arm through the leather strap and gave Ryann a mock salute, "Aye, aye, Captain."

"Come on, let's go," Ryann said, trying to suppress a smile while rolling his eyes. Side by side, the two friends started down the trail to Myraddin.

Drake's eyes grew wide as he sank into Lake Dora. He acted instinctively, trying to survive by flailing his arms up and down. It took a few seconds to fully grasp the idea that he was breathing in air instead of water and that he wasn't going to drown. That calming feeling only lasted a moment. The shimmery gold fluid he was passing through quickly faded to a dull gray. As it did, he began to see shapes appear and disappear all around him: first Aunt Belial, then Lord Ekron, then a fire-breathing dragon. He tried to close his eyes, but the images wouldn't go away. Thrashing about, he pushed and kicked at the figures. They remained, but then they began laughing, their eerie sounds echoing all around him. His feet hit something hard and Drake felt relieved to gain some sort of balance. An instant later his solid footing began crumbling like rotten floorboards as he dropped out of "the goo," as he would later call it, into Aeliana.

Drake's first moments in the new land mirrored those of survival. He gasped for air, checked his body for any injury, and then looked frantically for anyone or anything that might be around. Ryann and Liddy were nowhere to be seen, nor were there any other immediate threats, so Drake concentrated on his surroundings.

Grass, bushes, and trees looked the same as at home, although the sky appeared overcast. He thought it might be a full moon, as he looked up at the source of the light. He quickly turned away, his eyes burning. It was like looking directly into the sun. Drake wiped his watery eyes and looked around again. Something was very odd about this place, but he couldn't figure out what it was. Drake never had a tan, but as he examined his hands and arms he noticed that they were much more pale than normal, almost white. Drake's eyes darted down to his shirt. "This is weird," he thought, "I put on a red shirt this morning and this one is gray." He looked at his jeans and noticed they had changed from blue to black. His senses heightened by these oddities, Drake slowly turned around, taking in every flowering plant, bush, and tree he could. None of them were green. All of the flowers were white or gray. Holding his hand up to block the intensity of the light, it dawned on Drake that this probably wasn't a moon. It was their sun. That meant those weren't shadows—it was their regular color. He suddenly realized the truth. There was no color here. That's why he had reasoned it was nighttime.

Voices off to his right broke his daze. Drake lunged for the bushes. Listening again, he identified the familiar voices of Ryann and Liddy. Making his way through dense underbrush, Drake began the tedious process of trying to move ahead without making a sound. By the time he reached them, they had turned away and were heading in another direction. Recalling Ryann had been here before, Drake decided to follow them and see where they would lead him.

Now that she knew it was real, Liddy peppered Ryann with questions about the fascinating new world they had entered. Preoccupied with answering her questions, Ryann failed to notice his ring's faint flickers of black. It seemed like only minutes until the two of them reached Lake Penwyn.

"How do you know it's the same lake?" Liddy asked, then quickly added, "Not that I don't believe you."

Ryann pointed. "Look across the lake. That's Glenys Falls. The last time I was here I saw the lake, but from atop the falls instead of here."

Crack.

"Did you hear that Liddy?" Ryann whirled around, peering into the bushes beside them.

"I didn't hear a thing. Except for the sounds of the waterfall—"

Crack.

Ryann held his staff out in front of them. "Who's there?" he cried out.

"I'm coming out, I'm coming out. Don't shoot," the familiar voice sputtered.

Lowering his arms, a smile spread across Ryann's face as the furry creature burst through the brush.

"Raz!"

The raccoon came scurrying up to him with what seemed to be a grin of his own, although, as he already knew, it was hard to tell on animals if they were actually smiling or not.

"Raz, I'm so glad to see you."

"Essy, it's no use hiding anymore," Raz called out over his shoulder. "He's caught us."

The leopard slinked her way over to them as if disappointed about being discovered.

Liddy's mouth dropped open, marveling at the animals' conversation.

"Hi, I'm Liddy," she interrupted, holding out her hand.

"Oh, I'm sorry," Ryann apologized, "this is my friend Liddy I told you about the last time I was here."

"Quite right, quite right. Glad to make your acquaintance," Raz grasped her hand with his paw.

Liddy stared at the furry paw in amazement before displaying a big grin. "The pleasure is mine," she replied politely.

When introductions were complete, Ryann quickly recounted the story of how they had arrived again. Both animals remained attentive until Ryann finished, then Essy spoke out, "Raz, don't you think we should be moving along to the Feast?"

"Oh my, yes!" Raz blurted out. "Do come with us. This will be so exciting…so exciting! Only once a year, you know."

When they were out of sight, Drake slipped out from beneath the brush. He was amazed at the sight of talking animals and wasn't sure yet what he needed to do to.

"Stop the one who seeks to bind me," Lord Ekron had commanded. He did know that it would involve Ryann, so he'd have to follow them and stay out of sight.

Drake stayed focused on the noisy foursome in front of him. Caught up in their conversation like long-lost friends, he knew they wouldn't see him, but he wanted to stay far enough back just to be sure. Drake was so intent on remaining quiet and unseen that the voice behind him froze him in fear.

"You have done well," uttered the deep voice.

Drake slowly turned around, hoping the pounding in his chest wasn't noticeable. "Lord Ekron, I didn't know you'd be here."

"I wouldn't have, young one, but you have provided the way."

"I did?" Drake asked, watching a wide grin spread across his mentor's dark face.

"I can only be in one place at a time, and the pathway from Earth to here opens infrequently and only for short periods of time. You followed Ryann and opened the way for me. Now I will be able to establish a portal deep in these woods that we can travel back and forth through."

Pride welled up within Drake at having done something well for Lord Ekron.

The dark angel murmured, "This is only the beginning. We have much to accomplish. You are only one. Step off the path with me and I'll tell you what must be done."

The foursome rounded the lake to see the setting sun at their backs reflecting brilliantly off the white stronghold in front of them. The chatting abruptly ended and an awkward pause settled upon the group until Liddy broke the silence.

"It's so beautiful."

"It is," Raz agreed. "Castle Myraddin is everything the Word intended for it to be."

"Look, up in the sky," Essy said, redirecting their attention.

Three blue full moons were spaced evenly across the sky in front of them.

"What does it mean?" Ryann asked the inevitable.

Raz answered, "It is the coming together of the Word. Once a year the three moons converge over the top of Castle Myradinn. That is when we are spoken to."

Ryann knew he had never seen anything so spectacular. He stood there frozen in place, mesmerized by the glowing blue moons gradually making their way toward one another.

"We had better get moving if we want to make the Feast," Essy said, breaking the silence.

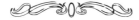

"*Pssst!*"

The sturdy dwarf stopped immediately and looked around. Normally he would have been focused on the moons and kept walking. However, in recent weeks he had begun to feel discontent with his home.

"Over here," the hushed voice called.

Looking off the path in the direction of the voice, he could barely see the outline of a human in the dimming light.

"Who is it?" the dwarf called back.

He slowly let down his guard as the young human with stiff red hair stayed in the shadows of the woods, off the path, but moved closer toward him.

"My name is Drake. Where are you off to in such a hurry?"

"To the castle, of course. Everyone knows that when the three blue moons come together we are to all gather for the Feast of the Word."

"Did the Word really say that *all* of you must gather? Maybe He meant *all* of you that are available?"

"That is what has been passed along from generation to generation. It has always been that way," the dwarf answered, then quickly added, "but I have not ever thought about it the way you asked."

"Are you happy where you live?" Drake asked

The dwarf hesitated, wondering if he had been talking aloud. "Not entirely."

"Doesn't the Word desire you to be happy?"

"I'm not sure if I've ever heard Him say so," answered the squatty, dark-bearded man. "But why wouldn't He?"

Drake peered into the eyes of the vulnerable dwarf, then delivered his conclusion, "Then maybe the Word would want you to come with me so that I can help you find a better place to live."

The dwarf recalled how he had been to the Feast every year for fifty years, yet still found himself in a shabby old house. Thinking he deserved better, he concluded that this was the answer he had been looking for.

The hand extending out of the darkening forest shocked him.

"Come with me," Drake said with an evil grin.

Taking his hand, the dwarf stepped off the path and into the darkness.

CHAPTER 9

Wonderful Words

RYANN AND LIDDY beamed with delight. They were experiencing a fantasy, previously lived out only through adventure books. Not wanting to miss a thing, they stumbled over themselves, looking in every direction as they tried to keep up with Raz and Essy.

The great hall of Castle Myraddin was bursting with activity. Echoes of roaring, barking, squealing, cooing, neighing, singing, and laughing resounded off the lofty peaked ceilings as everyone made their way into the hall. Ryann was amazed at the pairs of animals conversing together—lions with zebras, foxes with rabbits, and bears with sheep. Back home they would have been eating one another. More amazing were the creatures that didn't exist back home: unicorns, fawns, pixies, elves, centaurs, and

dryads. Of course, there were humans—at least he assumed they were—but nothing appeared very special about any of them.

"Look!" Liddy cried out, tugging on Ryann's arm. Off to the side, down in front, a white dragon sat back on its haunches, perfectly still and stately. Ryann would have thought it was a large statue, except for the wet nostrils that rhythmically flared in and out.

"Is it safe?" Liddy asked as she caught up to Essy and pointed in the direction of the dragon.

"You mean Sorcha?" Essy grinned. "That all depends upon how you define *safe*."

Having adjusted to a roomful of talking animals and up until now purely mythical creatures, Ryann looked ahead of Raz and Essy to a few open spots at the bulky wooden tables. The great hall was just what he would have imagined an ancient castle would look like. Roughly chiseled stones formed the massive walls that soared skyward into the darkness. Red and orange rays from the setting sun splashed through large, stained glass circular windows midway up the walls, creating a banner of colors streaming to the floor. Coupled with two-foot tall, thick green candles, this was the only light for the room.

"Have you ever seen such a spread of food, Ryann?" Liddy asked, looking up and down their long row of tables.

"Only at Thanksgiving or Christmas dinners. But never this much variety."

Shiny golden bowls spilled over with fruits of every color. Ryann marveled at how large and fresh the grapes, bananas, oranges, apples, pears, peaches, and strawberries looked. Then there were some other odd-shaped things he assumed to be fruit but had never seen before. He thought he'd have to try the pinkish, oblong fruit that looked like the fruit he had seen on the Tree of Life. He wondered if it would taste sweet or sour. Other bowls of varying sizes were heaped full of vegetables, steaming rice and noodles, mashed potatoes, olives, nuts, and breads. Breathing in the tantalizing aromas made Ryann's stomach growl in desire, having been deprived of food since breakfast early that morning.

Dong!

The clanging brass gong interrupted the roar of conversation and the great hall grew silent.

Ryann and Liddy looked out of the corners of their eyes to see what everyone else was doing and bowed their heads to mimic those around them. At first, Ryann kept one eye open to see if someone would pray like his family did at home around the dinner table. Silence. Then he shut both eyes, shifting back and forth from one foot to the other. He was tempted to raise his head and look around, but knew he didn't dare at this point. Then…

Donggg!—Donggg!—Donggg!

The gong reverberated throughout the cavernous hall in three lengthy blows. Heads rose in unison and everyone sat down. Ryann and Liddy imitated the others, not wanting to seem out of place, while the first ones seated began attending to the food.

"Here you go, young man," snorted a jovial warthog Ryann hadn't noticed sitting to his right. He tried to ignore the wet snout staring him in the face as he took a bowl of puffy rolls and then passed them along.

"Would you mind passing me a quant?" the warthog grunted, pointing past him while stuffing three rolls into his mouth.

"A what?" Ryann turned in the direction the warthog had pointed. One of the huge bowls of towering fruit was off to his left, in front of Liddy.

"Liddy, pass me a quant, please," Ryann said loud enough for those in front and beside him to hear.

"A wha..?" she started, giving him a quizzical glare.

Raz came to her rescue, his paw darting out to retrieve one of the pink-colored oval-shaped things and handing it to Liddy. Ryann passed it along.

"Name's Grotch," the warthog chortled before chomping into the quant.

"I'm Ryann. It's a pleasure to meet you, Grotch." He winced as the warthog devoured the fruit, leaving a slimy trail of pink goo from his snout to the corner of his mouth. For some reason the fruit didn't have the same appeal it had moments before.

An hour or so later, the initial wave of raucous hunger had subsided and was replaced by calm pleasantries and after-dinner conversation. Liddy had changed places with Raz and was talking intently with Essy. Grotch let out a loud belch. Ryann suppressed a groan, moving closer to Raz to avoid the inevitable stench.

"So, Raz," he rushed into conversation so as not to offend the warthog, "what happens next?"

Raz pointed to the highest circular window down front at the peak of the upward sloping cathedral-like room. "When the three blue moons converge and become one, their light will flood through that window and fill the room. It is then that the Word will speak to us."

"What do we do while the Word is speaking?"

Raz looked at Ryann in disbelief, started to answer, then stopped himself. He finally replied, nodding his head. "You'll know what to do, Ryann."

Before Ryann could ask another question, loud whispers rippled across the room. He looked skyward, then tugged at Liddy and pointed. The three blue moons were entering the main window from different directions. All eyes locked on to the window, awaiting the glorious event that occurred once a year. Even Grotch's pungent bodily functions went silent.

Drawing together like magnets, the blue moons loomed larger and larger, until they filled the center window and glowed as one. At first, Ryann peered into the stream of blue light, but the intense brightness became too much and he found himself slowly bowing, then kneeling, and finally lying on the ground. The light was so bright and glorious that the reflection off the dingy stone floor forced him to clamp his eyes shut. He felt an odd mixture of fear and peace at the same time; fear at the sheer power pressing in all around him, yet peace, knowing that this power was good.

The voice came from the light, but instead of hearing it clearly through his ears, Ryann tingled inside as it came straight into his chest.

> *To be praised are you who do not walk in the counsel*
>   *of the wicked,*
> *Nor step off the pathway to the Word.*
> *Your delight is in Me and on My words you meditate*
>   *day and night.*
> *You are like a tree firmly planted by streams of water,*
>   *yielding fruit in its season. Your leaves do not wither.*
> *Whatever you do will prosper.*
> *Not so with the wicked.*
> *They will be like chaff, which the wind drives away.*
> *They will not be able to stand with you.*
> *For My ways are your ways,*
>   *but the ways of the wicked will perish.*

Sweat beaded on his face as Ryann pictured the words being etched into his mind. Straining on each syllable, Ryann yearned to absorb more of the pure words and light.

> *I am everlasting, the Creator of the ends of the earth.*
> *I will not grow weary, and my understanding no one*
>   *can fathom.*
> *I give strength to the weary and increase the power*
>   *of the weak.*
> *Even yearlings grow tired and weary,*
>   *and young creatures stumble and fall;*
>   *but those who trust in Me will renew their strength.*
> *They will soar on wings like eagles;*
>   *they will run and not grow weary,*
>   *they will walk and not be faint.*

The sound of howling winds swirled around the room. Ryann continued to lie face down, his eyes scrunched shut, as he felt the presence of the light rising from his back. Limp and drained of any strength, Ryann wondered if he'd be able to get himself up. He opened his eyes and raised his head enough to see the entire room awakening as if coming out of a long hibernation. Liddy was on one knee next to him.

"Can you believe that Ryann?" Liddy breathed heavily. "It felt like the words were searing into my insides."

"That's the way I felt, too." Ryann pushed himself up into a sitting position.

Their eyes locked, both thought it, but Liddy said it first, "Your face...it's glowing."

"Yes, indeed," Raz quipped. "You cannot look into the face of the Word, yet we are all still touched by His presence."

"Is it always this way?"

"It is. Then the castle scribe writes down the spoken word so that we can preserve the truth for those who could not be here in person."

"I don't think I'll ever forget this day," Liddy said.

"Ahh," Essy purred into the conversation, "the words I remember so well are from when I was a young cat, just out of the litter. They became more meaningful to me as I read them when I was older."

Liddy was enjoying her new friendship with the leopard. "Oh, do go on, Essy. It feels so right to hear the truth."

Essy continued, "The Word spoke it:

> In the beginning was the Word, and the Word was with God, and the Word was God.
> He was in the beginning with God.
> All things came into being by Him, and apart from Him nothing came into being that has come into being.
> In Him was life, and the life was the light of men.

And the light shines in the darkness, and the darkness did not comprehend it."

"That's it!" Ryann exclaimed, putting the pieces together, "the Word and God are one and the same."

Raz nodded approvingly. "That is correct, Ryann."

"He catches on quick for a male of the species," Essy winked at Liddy.

"Yeah, yeah, yeah, I've had a lot on my mind, like I still have to find the King's sword," Ryann replied sarcastically, "and I'm not even sure which king."

Liddy gasped. "Ryann, your ring—it's gold!"

"Oh, no!" Ryann cried out. "Not now. There's too much I want to do here."

"I'm sorry, Ryann. His timing is not our timing," Raz said with conviction, as if he had experienced similar situations.

"Where can we find water around here? I'm being called back home."

Liddy corrected him, "You mean, *we're* being called back home."

"Right as usual," Ryann rolled his eyes. "Raz, can you and Essy escort us outside to the closest water?"

Raz responded royally, "It would be an honor."

The four made their way through the castle corridors, with Ryann and Liddy in the middle and Raz and Essy on the outside. Liddy began to tear up at the thought of leaving the big cat.

"Oh, Essy," she cried, wrapping her arms around the leopard and resting her head on the smooth fur. "I do hope it isn't too long until we meet again."

Liddy felt the deep purr vibrate against her ear. "There is still much to be done. I'm sure we'll see each other again soon," Essy replied.

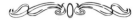

Following the dark figure through the forest mystified the middle-aged dwarf. First, that this Drake fellow could see so well to find his way through, and second, that he was even following him in the first place. The sounds of their plodding through scrub brush mixed with his heavy breathing as the shorter-legged dwarf tried to keep up the pace. The farther they traveled from the path, the more he wondered about his decision.

"We're almost there," Drake encouraged.

Breaking free of the confines of the forest, the two entered a clearing lit by the dancing flames of scattered torches.

"This can all be yours," Drake announced, stretching his arms out wide. "Go on, go take a look for yourself."

Rushing across the small grassy meadow, the dwarf came to a newly crafted wooden door, built into the base of a towering rock hill. The hill dwarfs, of which he was one, were used to living in and around the sides of hills and mountains. The dwarf's face grinned in anticipation as he turned the doorknob.

"This could be the perfect place I've never had," he muttered to himself.

Drake folded his arms and waited. He knew it wouldn't be long. Despite the drawback of a colorless world, he liked being in Aeliana. If everyone were as easy to sway as this dwarf, he'd rise to the top in no time. "It's time to pay a visit to Ryann," he thought, throwing the black cloak over his back and disappearing into the darkness of the Western woods to find the portal back to Mount Dora.

A few moments later the dwarf reappeared. "It's perfect!" he cried out. Scanning the edge of the dark forest for signs of the gift giver, he was met with a murky white fog creeping across the meadow toward him. A chill ran down the nape of his neck, and he quickly stepped inside and locked the door.

CHAPTER 10

Doldrums
& Doubt

RYANN DIDN'T THINK he'd ever get used to the travel to and from Aeliana. The bubbling gold circle, taking that leap of faith, and the radiating glow while slowly passing from one world to the other would never get boring. This time, he had the pleasure of watching Liddy's newfound fascination all the way back. Sharing the experience and having her eyes opened to the reality of Raz, Essy, Aeliana, and now the Word, had him bursting with joy. One of his best friends had gone from an unbeliever to a believer, and it made the pain he had felt over her skepticism bearable.

They landed in Liddy's backyard in the same manner they had popped into Aeliana—feet seemingly dangling in mid-air and then a gentle fall into the thick St. Augustine grass.

"What time is it?" Liddy asked, glancing about for Drake.

"It's still about the same time it was when we left," Ryann assured her. "No telling where Drake is now. Time slows down almost to a standstill here while we're in Aeliana."

"You expect me to believe that?"

Ryann's exuberant face fell flat.

Liddy winced. "Ryann, I'm so sorry," she said, watching his shoulders follow his face and slump in dejection. "It's just so natural for me to doubt anything that's not scientific or in a textbook."

Ryann, eyes downcast, picked at the grass awkwardly. There was an uneasy silence until he had completely worn away a bare spot in the grassy patch he was pulling.

Still looking down, Ryann responded, "I'm just hurt that you don't believe me, Liddy. It's like…like, you're rejecting me."

Ryann glanced up briefly to see a side of Liddy he hadn't seen before. Her eyes were shiny and wet, like she was on the verge of tears.

"Ryann, I'm sorry," she said again. "It's not you I'm rejecting, it's what you were telling me…and now that I've experienced it, I feel awful that I didn't believe it in the first place."

Ryann shifted uncomfortably. "Well, I'm just glad you could come there with me and see it for yourself."

Liddy shook her head slowly as a small tear ran down her cheek. "But that's just it," she spoke softly. "Terell believed you all along and he's never even been to Aeliana. I had to see it to believe it."

"Liddy," her mom called from the back door, "it's almost time for supper."

"Ya know," Ryann said lightheartedly, "we've probably been talking together, here in our time, longer than we were actually away."

"Ha! You're probably right," Liddy smiled.

"Liddy? Dinner!"

"Coming, Mom."

"No hard feelings, Liddy," Ryann said as they walked back toward the house. "I'm really glad we were able to go together. See you tomorrow in class."

"See ya," Liddy managed meekly as Ryann peddled away.

A wadded-up ball of paper whooshed through the air, barely missing the boy's head. More than ever, the laughter and fooling around before class reflected the fact that in another three weeks school would be out for the summer.

"Ha! Missed!" yelled the boy sarcastically.

Ryann made his way through the ruckus toward his desk, looking over his shoulder to avoid the next fastball. There was no way he could have steered clear of the outstretched leg.

"Whoa!" Ryann yelled, as he and his books flew forward through the air. He landed with a heavy thud, his textbooks and papers scattering about. Laughter erupted all around him, and Ryann knew without looking that only one person could be responsible.

"What's the matter, clumsy?" Drake asked with mock concern. "Trip over a shoelace?" The hootin' and hollerin' died down to pockets of snickering onlookers.

Gritting his teeth, he slowly lifted himself up off the floor and turned to face Drake. Fists clenched, Ryann glared at the sneering class bully seated in front of him.

Both boys took center stage as the room sank into silent anticipation.

"Hey, everyone," Drake mocked, "I think he's a little angry."

Ryann felt his chest heaving. He had never been in a fight before, but more than anything he wanted to slug Drake with everything he had.

"Like I always say, put up or shut up," Drake began lecturing the class, "and it looks to me like—"

Ryann didn't let Drake finished his sentence. Ryann thrust himself forward, like he was shot out of a cannon, pushing the larger boy off his chair. The move caught Drake completely off-balance. With his finger wagging in the air to make his point to the class, Drake found himself staring at the ceiling, feet sticking straight up.

The loud "Ooohh" in unison from his classmates was a mixture of shock and excitement, like the approval of fireworks on the Fourth of July. Drake got to his feet as the door slammed and Ms. Buttlework's nasal voice wallowed, "And just what exactly is going on here?"

Hurried whispers began throughout the room, and one little voice eeked out above the rest, "It's Drake's fault; he started it."

Ms. Buttlework waddled over to the scene. "Is that true, Drake?"

Nearly famous for always skirting the edge of trouble without ever being caught, Drake found himself at a loss. Ready to give himself up, he shook his hand at the burning sensation coming from his finger. Glancing down at the glowing red dragon on his ring, Drake recalled the special gift Lord Ekron had given him. Even though Lord Ekron had told him not to use it in this world, Drake didn't care—he wasn't about to get in trouble if he could help it.

"Well, Drake?" the teacher's nasal voice asked again.

Lifting his hand up slightly, Drake pointed the ring in the direction of Ms. Buttlework, looked into her eyes, and repeated to himself, "It's Ryann's fault, he started it. It's Ryann's fault, he started it…"

Ms. Buttlework blinked her eyes a few times then turned to Ryann and stated matter-of-factly, "Mister Watters, it's obvious to me that you started this. I want to see you after class."

Ryann looked at her in disbelief, his arms limp at his side.

"Seats, everyone!" the nasal voice rang out. Everyone scurried to their places, including a smirking Drake.

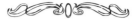

"Ryann, I'm really quite surprised at you," Ms. Buttlework began. The class had long since emptied and Ryann stood in front of his teacher's desk.

"I consider you to be one of the leaders in the class, and to have you starting fights…" She shook her head.

"But Ma'am, it wasn't my—" He started to say *fault* and thought of his father, a graduate of the Naval Academy. He had always taught him to be accountable for your actions. But he hadn't really started it, had he?

She waved him off and continued, "We simply can't have that kind of distraction in the classroom. According to school guidelines, you should be expelled."

Ryann shifted uncomfortably.

"However, since I've never had any trouble with you before and no one was hurt, I'm going to have you serve a week of detention after school." She paused, acting as if she had just given him a birthday present.

"Uh…thank you?" Ryann said meekly.

"I'll call your parents to let them know what happened and that your detention will start immediately."

"Yes, Ma'am." Ryann answered dejectedly as he turned to walk back to his seat. "Just great," he muttered under his breath. "How am I going to explain this to Mom and Dad?"

Detention lasted for one hour. Scuffling his feet along the ground, Ryann made his way toward the bike compound. It was completely empty now, except for his bicycle. Terell and Liddy had long since departed. Ryann pushed his bike out of the fenced area and peddled home alone.

The usual dinnertime chatter about events of the day had been reduced to uncomfortable silence. Ryann felt like he was eating in the library as he tried to keep his fork from scraping against his plate. Henry and Alyson had excused themselves quickly, and now it was just Ryann and his parents. His father broke the silence.

"So, son, would you care to explain how this all happened?"

"No excuse, sir?" Ryann half answered, half questioned, using one of his father's five basic responses he had been expected to reply with as a plebe at the Academy.

"No, son, we really want to know. Ms. Buttlework was very upset about a fight breaking out in her class."

Ryann poked at his food. "There's this bully in our class, Drake. Drake Dunfellow, and he tripped me on the way to my seat."

"And?" His father arched a brow.

"He did it on purpose. You should have seen it. I went flying through the air, books and papers everywhere."

"And that's when you started the fight?"

"He started teasing me in front of the whole class, Dad. That's when I pushed him."

"I see." Mr. Watters rubbed his chin. "So, would you do the same thing again?"

"I don't know what else I could have done," Ryann answered. "Everyone would have thought I was a wuss if I didn't do anything."

"Oh, so this is more about everyone else than about the fight?"

"No sir. I mean, yes sir. I...oh, I don't know. It seemed to make a lot of sense at the time. I was just so angry," Ryann emphasized his point by stabbing hard at the meat on his plate.

"Ryann, it's okay to get angry."

"It is?"

"Sure. But it's what we do with that anger that can lead to a positive result, or in this case a negative one."

"Well, what else could I have done?"

"You could have just picked up your things and continued to your desk. Then when the teacher came in you could have let her know what happened."

"Dad, everyone would call me a snitch."

"Then you could have just let it go. Which do you think would be harder to do, push this Drake fellow or sit down?"

"Sit down." Ryann pulled his fork out of the meat. "I was so angry, I wanted to punch him, but that seemed really wrong, so I just pushed him instead."

Mrs. Watters flinched.

"Pushing him was a better choice, Ryann," his father continued. "But your anger had more control over you than you did over it."

"You're right, Dad."

"My experience has shown me that most of the time bullies are just looking for attention from others and to get a reaction out of the person they pick on. He probably would have been very disappointed if you had just gone to your seat."

"You think so?"

"I'm pretty sure, but don't take my word for it. Go get your Bible."

Ryann looked from his dad to his mom to see if he was serious. Then, he popped up and raced up the stairs to his room. In no time he was back in his seat, breathing heavily.

"Now, open it to Proverbs 25."

Ryann was very familiar with Proverbs. It was smack dab in the middle of the Bible and written by the wisest man who ever lived, Solomon.

"Now read verses 21 and 22."

Ryann began aloud, "If your enemy is hungry, give him food to eat; if he is thirsty, give him water to drink. In doing this, you will heap burning coals on his head, and the Lord will reward you."

Ryann looked up quizzically. "I don't know about the feeding part, but I like the idea of heaping burning coals on Drake's head."

"Ryann Watters!" his mom piped in.

"Just kidding, Mom." Ryann smiled for the first time. Turning back to his dad he asked, "What does it mean?"

"It means we should be kind to our enemies. That's the last thing they're expecting. And, by returning good for bad, we may cause them to change."

"Do you really think so? Drake's pretty bad."

His dad pressed him further. "What does the last line say?"

"That the Lord will reward you."

"That's right. It doesn't say they have to change for us to receive the reward; we just have to do our part."

"Wow…that's neat! I didn't realize you could find the answers to everyday problems in the Bible." Ryann beamed.

"You'd be amazed," Mr. Watters confirmed. "But that doesn't excuse what happened in class today. You need to apologize to Ms. Buttlework tomorrow for your behavior, and until you finish serving your detention this week, no hanging out with friends. You come right home from school."

Ryann stared down at his food again.

"Ryann, we love you," his mom said. "If we didn't, we wouldn't be spending this time with you helping you work through it."

"Yes, ma'am. Thanks." Even as he said it, he thought, "That's the second time today I've said 'thanks' for getting in trouble."

"Now, why don't you excuse yourself and head up to your room and do your homework?" Ryann's dad said, concluding the matter.

"Yes, sir."

Ryann walked up the stairs with new energy. Finding the sword still seemed a long way off, but without any distractions for the week, there was going to be more time to try and figure it out.

CHAPTER 11

Double
Vision

AT FIRST, RYANN thought a week of detention at school and restriction at home would not be so bad. By the end of Wednesday's punishment, he was beginning to have his doubts. As he hopped onto his bike for the two-mile trip home, Ryann's thoughts were focused on his failure to find the sword.

"I'm no closer to finding the sword now than I was a month ago," he thought. "Gabriel never gave a time limit, but at this rate I'll be thirty before I find it, if ever," he bemoaned as he turned onto Donnelly Street. "Who am I trying to kid? I'm not the one who should be doing this."

Peddling just fast enough to keep himself upright, Ryann sluggishly continued in the direction of his house. As he approached Eleventh Street, an idea popped into his head. Instead of turning toward his house, Ryann continued going straight and quickened his pace. His parents had said to come home right after school, but first he needed to go the long way past the church.

He coasted to a stop around back at the familiar sight of Noah Johnson asleep across the wooden bench.

"Noah!" Ryann called out dropping his bike. "I've got something I need to ask you."

Noah didn't move until Ryann was standing right in front of him and then it was only one eye that popped open.

"I haven't seen you for a while, Ryann. How's the search coming?"

"Fine, fine," Ryann replied automatically. "Well…actually, terrible. That's why I stopped by."

Noah sat up, nodding his head, a pleasant smile on his face, "And…you thought ol' Noah might be able to cheer you up?"

"Kind of. It's a long story and I need to get home pretty quick. Let's just say I have no clue on what to do next. I'm thinking maybe God should have picked someone else to find the sword."

Noah patted Ryann reassuringly, "Didn't Gabriel answer that question for you?"

"He said God doesn't make mistakes, but…it's taking so long."

"Ahh, so you don't really think God's made a mistake, you just don't like the timing."

Ryann scratched his head. "Okay, so maybe I can believe that He picked me on purpose, but why would He ask me to do something and then have it take so long to do it?"

"God does things on His schedule, not ours, Ryann. Do you remember the story of Abraham and Sarah? God promised them a son and then Sarah didn't have him until she was ninety years old."

"I bet they had their doubts," Ryann offered.

"They sure did," Noah said. "Abraham and Sarah both laughed at the idea of having children when they were that old because they thought it was impossible. But with God, all things are possible."

Ryann started to look at his watch, knowing his parents would be expecting him soon. The white glow of his ring diverted his attention. He knew that Noah must be telling him the truth and decided to risk asking a few more questions.

"Well, what's the purpose in making it take so long?"

Noah's blue eyes twinkled. "If everything happened when we wanted it to or because of our efforts, who do you think would take all the credit?"

"We would," Ryann answered.

"Who do you think got the credit when Sarah had a baby at age ninety?"

"God."

"Exactly," Noah nodded. "God uses time and circumstances to teach us lessons about ourselves, help us realize that He is taking care of us, and to bring us closer to Him."

Ryann considered what Noah said carefully. "So, you're saying that if I thought everything I did was a result of my efforts...then, I wouldn't learn anything about myself and that God is involved in my life?"

"What do you think, Ryann?"

"You're probably right. Most likely I'd just think how smart or good I was and not think much about God at all."

Noah smiled and continued, "And what if things didn't happen like you wanted them to? Then how would you feel?"

"I guess, a little like I do now...frustrated. And I'd probably blame God."

"God's not trying to frustrate you, Ryann, but whatever situation you find yourself in you need to ask yourself—what is God trying to teach me? He didn't create people just to sit back and see what they would do. He cares about us and is doing things around us all the time."

"Wow," Ryann announced, throwing his hands up in the air. "I never thought about God that way before. I always thought things just happened, and if they didn't turn out like I wanted them to, it was just bad luck or that I did something wrong."

Noah leaned forward, his face kind, but more serious than before. "Ryann," he almost whispered, as if letting him in on a big secret, "because God loves us, life won't turn out the way we planned—" He paused to let Ryann carefully consider each word before finishing, "—it will turn out better."

Ryann broke his stare at the old man and looked at his watch again. "Oh boy, I need to get home. Thanks for all the good advice, Noah. I'm feeling a lot better about things already."

As he hopped up on his bike, Noah had a few last words. "Remember, Ryann, things don't happen by accident. For instance, have you ever wondered why your name is spelled with two *n*'s?"

"As a matter of fact, I have," he answered as Noah laid back down on the bench, shifting a little to get more comfortable, then closed his eyes. Ryann waited to see if Noah would say anything else. He was greeted with silence and a slow grin spreading across the old man's face. Shrugging his shoulders, Ryann turned and pedaled away, yelling over his shoulder as he sped off, "Thanks again!"

Encouraged by his time with Noah, Ryann sat at his desk pouring over page after page of his Bible, trying to find some clue on what to do next. He scanned up and down, determined not to get impatient waiting on God. He was so intent on his task that the voice of his dad entering the room startled him.

"So, Ryann, how's the homework going?"

"Oh, uh, great, Dad. I finished it a while ago. I'm reading my Bible now."

"Really?" his dad asked somewhat skeptically. "What are you learning?"

"To be honest, Dad, it's a little frustrating. I'm trying to find certain things, and, well, they just seem to stay, uh, hidden."

"Ryann, your mom and I were a little worried about you with the incident at school, but seeing you so diligent about reading the Bible, that's encouraging. I'm proud of you, son."

Ryann shifted in his seat. "Thanks, Dad."

"I'll tell you what, Ryann," his dad beamed, "I saw a Bible software package for your computer at the store the other day. It had the entire Bible on it; maps, cross-references, and everything. If you want, I can pick it up for you. I bet it would help you find whatever it is you're looking for."

"Wow, Dad!" Ryann cheered. "That'd be great."

"It's a deal, then. I'll get it for you tomorrow," he said as he closed the door, "and don't stay up too late reading."

Ryann was elated. In the morning he would be able to tell Terell and Liddy. He could only hope that maybe his mom and dad would let them come over after school for a few minutes.

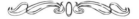

"Thirty minutes, Ryann, that's all," Ryann's father said as he handed him the Bible software. "Having your friends over is a reward for the great attitude you've had all week."

"Thanks, Dad, I'll call Terell and Liddy in just a minute. First I need to load this software and make sure it's ready to go. I don't want to waste a second of the time."

"That's good planning, son," Mr. Watters patted Ryann on the shoulder before heading back downstairs.

The phone call to Liddy was quick and to the point. Ryann's stomach began churning as he dialed Terell. He hadn't spoken to him since Terell betrayed him by telling Drake everything about the sword and Word.

"Hello?"

"Hey, Terell, this is Ryann."

After a moment of silence, Terell admitted quickly, "Ryann, I'm so glad you called, man. I've been feeling awful about what happened with Drake."

"That's okay, Terell, everything's turned out fine."

"Thanks for understanding, dude...I've been feeling this way for days."

"Hey—better subject—you need to get over here in thirty minutes. I think I'm on the verge of a major breakthrough, and I need Liddy and you to help."

"Cool, I'll tell my mom," Terell said, his spirits obviously rising. "See you in a few."

By the time Terell and Liddy had made their way over to Ryann's house, he had figured out the program and had the entry screen pulled up and waiting. Ryann sat at the keyboard while Terell and Liddy pushed in as close as they could get on either side.

Liddy was the first to speak up. "Have you figured it out yet? How does it work?"

"Are you kidding? I didn't want to start without you guys. The directions say to enter a word or group of words, and the program will search for a list of all the matches."

"Well, let's get started," Liddy said, pushing in closer. "We only have twenty-five minutes left!"

"Okay, okay, let's start with the obvious, *sword*," Ryann said. He clicked away on the keyboard, then pressed Enter.

Terell shrieked. "Wow! Sword shows up 1,539 times."

Ryann hummed. "Let's back up and try *word*." He typed it in.

"Ugh," moaned Terell, "23,101 times!"

"I wonder..." Liddy paused.

"What?" both boys said together, while turning to look at her.

"What if you put in two words, like *word* and *sword*?"

"How do I do that?" Ryann asked.

"Type in *word*, then a plus sign, and then *sword*."

Ryann quickly did what she said. "That's it! *Word* and *sword* only show up 43 times together."

Their excitement was short-lived, however, as they looked through the verses one by one, not seeing anything of significance. It was Liddy who finally broke the silence with only ten minutes left before they would have to leave.

"I can't imagine there's more than one verse that would fit the description of what we're looking for. Maybe we need to add another word."

Ryann scratched his head. "But what?"

"Think Ryann, is there anything Raz, Essy, or anyone else has said to you that might give us a clue?"

"I can't think of a thing."

"It's probably something that has to do with you. I mean you are the one that was chosen," Liddy added.

"Mmm, I like fishing and riding my bike. Oh, I don't know, Liddy," Ryann sighed, the air escaping out of his lips like a slow leak in a bicycle tire.

"Come on, Ryann, think," Liddy pleaded.

"Wait a second. Noah said something to me the other day after I stopped by to say hello."

Terell spoke up for the first time in nearly fifteen minutes. "What was it?"

"Well, it was actually a question. I only remember it because it was kinda strange. He asked me if I knew why my name was spelled with two *n*'s."

"Do you?" Liddy asked.

"No, I asked my parents once and my mom said she decided to spell it that way while she was filling out my birth certificate."

"You have two *n*'s in your first name and two *t*'s in your last name," Liddy noted. "Why not add *two* to the search list?"

"Okay," Ryann said, quickly typing in *word, sword,* and *two.*

Terell moaned. "Zero matches. Now what?"

Liddy was staring intently at the screen, then her bright, blue eyes lit up. "Ryann, try *double* instead of *two*."

"All right," Ryann said unconvincingly. "But this is our last chance. Our thirty minutes are just about up." He deleted *two* and typed in *double*.

For a moment the only sound in the room was the hum of the computer, then the silence was broken by the eruption of cheers.

"There's only one match," Ryann said giddily. "It's gotta be it!"

Liddy nudged him. "Pull it up, quick, before we have to go."

"I'm hurrying, I'm hurrying," Ryann answered as he double-clicked on the verse, Hebrews 4:12.

"Ryann, it's time for Terell and Liddy to go!" his mom yelled from down in the kitchen.

"They're on their way down!"

Liddy quickly read through the verse when it popped up onto the screen, "For the word of God is living and active. Sharper than any double-edged sword, it penetrates even to dividing soul and spirit, joints and marrow; it judges the thoughts and attitudes of the heart."

"Thanks for coming guys—you'd better go." Ryann said. "Look the verse up at home and let me know if you figure out any clues from it. Hebrews 4:12."

Ryann got his Bible out and highlighted the verse. He read through it word by word, trying to find the hidden meaning. Something was familiar to him about it.

Ryann sat up in bed. The only light in the room came from dull-white moon rays peeking through the blinds. He knew it must be the middle of the night as he made his way over to his desk and turned on his small lamp. His Bible was still open to the same verse, and he read through it one more time to be sure.

"That has to be it," he whispered to himself as he read through the verse a second time, his finger stopping on the key words he remembered from Aeliana. "Wait until I share this with Terell and Liddy."

CHAPTER 12

Virtue & Vice

"BOY, YOU LOOK tired," Liddy said as Ryann came strolling into class the next day.

Ryann slid behind a desk between his two friends. He had tossed and turned in bed for hours last night after figuring out the significance of the verse. The haunting face staring back at him in the bathroom mirror this morning startled him. Ryann rubbed at the dark circles under his eyes, but they wouldn't wash away. He had been far too excited to sleep and wanted his friends to experience just a touch of it themselves. As the bell rang, students jerked in and around desks, and Ryann blurted out to his friends, "I figured out where the sword is."

Terell and Liddy faced him, mouths agape, as Ms. Buttlework began the class. Ryann pretended to be paying attention to the teacher, a very serious look on his face. Inside, though, he was smiling to himself. He knew his friends would be wondering the entire class period about what he would have to say.

Three grueling hours later, Liddy and Terell were ready to burst in anticipation as their last class before lunch ended and found them practically running for the lunchroom.

"No way!" Terell exclaimed as Ryann finished recounting the puzzle he had solved the night before. Ryann had taken up almost the entire break to give them every last detail, the most important of which was that he had awoken in the middle of the night recalling two places on either side of Castle Myraddin: the Joynnted Knolls and the Marrow Mountains. That had to be it—the sword was divided, or in this case hidden, somewhere between "joints and marrow," like the verse said.

Liddy, the most practical of the trio, was the one to throw cold water on the episode. "So, Ryann, how many miles do you think there are between the Joynnted Knolls and the Marrow Mountains?"

Ryann's forehead scrunched up, "Ohhhh, probably twenty-five square miles."

"Well, I don't want to be the bearer of bad news," she said, "but don't you think it's going to be hard to find a sword in an area the size of Orlando?"

All was silent as Ryann stared straight ahead. "Ya know, Liddy, I think if God has brought us this far, we can trust Him to take us the rest of the way."

"You tell her, homeboy," Terell said smiling and nodding his head.

Liddy rolled her eyes. "But how are you going to do it, Ryann?"

"That's just it, Liddy, it's not about me. He's the one we need to focus on. To be quite honest, I'm looking forward to seeing how He reveals the location to us."

His optimism was short lived. A few weeks later, nothing new had happened, and it was now the last week of school. Ryann looked over toward his desk as he walked out of his bedroom. The scoured pages of his Bible were wrinkled and worn from searching late into the night. He hadn't found a thing. Ryann slammed his door in frustration and stomped heavily down the stairs.

"What's wrong?" his mother asked as he searched through the cupboard for his favorite cereal.

"I don't want to talk about it," Ryann sulked.

"That's fine, Ryann, but just know your dad and I are available if you decide you do."

At school things didn't get much better. A low roar of conversation with occasional high-pitched squeals filled the hallways as the excitement of the final week of classes permeated the air. Ryann trudged down the hallway, avoiding anyone he knew. Numerous questions raced around in his head as he rounded the corner and ran smack into Terell.

"Geez, Terell, can't you watch where you're going?" Ryann snapped.

"Uhh, sorry, Ryann."

"If you'd pay more attention, things like this wouldn't happen," Ryann said as he stooped down to pick up a book he dropped in the collision.

"Hey dude, I said I was sorry," Terell said again, staring as Ryann walked away. Shaking his head in disbelief, Terell continued on to his first-period class.

By Thursday, things hadn't gotten much better. With the last day of school only a few hours off, Ryann should have been as happy as his classmates. Instead, he sat glumly in his room staring at the now closed Bible lying on the desk in front of him. The soft knock on his door startled him.

"May I come in?" asked his father.

"Yes, sir."

Ryann didn't turn around but heard his bed sink down under the weight of his father. Ryann didn't feel like talking. The ticking of his wall clock kept the room from being totally silent until his father finally spoke.

"Your mother and I have noticed you haven't been your usual self, Ryann, especially during this last week of school."

It was a statement of fact, not a question, so Ryann didn't answer.

"Anything you'd like to talk about?"

"Not really, it's just—" Ryann stopped, not sure if he wanted to continue or not.

"Just what?"

Ryann chose his words carefully because he still didn't want to alert his parents about Aeliana. "Well, I was so excited about everything I've been reading in the Bible. It seemed so alive, but now—"

"Now things don't seem to be happening like you want them too?" his dad finished his sentence for him.

Ryann slowly swiveled around in his chair and raised his head to meet his dad's gaze. "Exactly, but how did you know?"

Mr. Watters scratched his chin, "Let me answer it this way, Ryann. Do you know how you like to play that computer game, *Sim City*?"

Ryann nodded, so he continued. "I've watched you take hours setting up the streets, houses, trees, rivers, and towns, and then watch as the little people work, play, and live in the environment you created."

Ryann continued nodding. That was one of his favorite games.

"Do you think one of those little people in the game can see the big picture of what is going on as well as you can on the screen?"

"No," Ryann quickly answered. "Sometimes I have to pick them up and move them somewhere else to help them out."

"And what happens if you sit back and don't do anything and just watch the game?"

"Eventually things start to break down, the roads don't get repaired, pollution sets in, and the people get very unhappy."

"Ryann, the reason people like that game is that they have control over everything that happens. They, in effect, get to act like a god. But the real God is so much more than that. Unlike the game, God is always actively involved in the world He created and always aware of what is going to happen next."

Ryann started to make the connection as his father continued.

"You may be frustrated by the circumstances around you or by things taking longer to happen than you'd like, but you can take comfort in knowing that God is already aware of what is going on in your life and is working out all things for your good."

"But everything doesn't always seem to work out good for me," Ryann replied.

"You said yourself, Ryann, that on your screen you can see what the people in the game can't. God does what He knows is best for us, even if it doesn't seem that way to us at the time. Sometimes we can look back on something we thought was bad, and it ends up that it either taught us something important about ourselves or helped someone else. There will be some things, though, that happen to us or to others, which we will never understand until we get to heaven. Those can be the most frustrating if we don't really believe that God loves us and controls everything."

"That seems to make sense, Dad, but what do you do about the frustrating part?"

"Just remember that our definition of good or bad isn't necessarily God's. I've found that if I focus more on what I know is pleasing to God instead of what is pleasing to me, then my outlook on seemingly bad things is a lot brighter."

For the first time in a week, a smile broke out across Ryann's face. "Thanks, Dad, that makes me feel a whole lot better."

"Glad to be of help. That's one of the reasons God made parents." Mr. Watters slapped his hands on his thighs as he got up to leave. "And, Ryann."

"Yes, Dad?"

"You still have to clean up your room." They both laughed as he closed the door behind him.

Ryann leaned back in his chair, by the bed, and reflected on the events of the day. A pit began to form in his stomach as he considered how he had treated everyone he had come into contact with, especially Terell. He was going to call his dad back in to talk about it but didn't want to have to explain anything else to him, so he opened the Bible software on his computer.

He hoped to see what the wisest man in the Bible had to say about using hurtful words with someone. Ryann narrowed his search to the book of Proverbs, then typed in *words*. Several verses popped up on his screen, with *words* highlighted in red, but his eyes naturally gravitated to the word *sword*. A smile spread across his face and Ryann shook his head in amazement as he recited the verse to himself, "Reckless words pierce like a sword, but the tongue of the wise brings healing." He meditated on the verse, repeating it to himself several times, as he thought about the "reckless words" he had said in anger to kids at school that day. Ryann knew what he needed to do. He needed to apologize to those kids whose feelings he had hurt and bring healing. That was the wise thing to do. After reading, a glimmer of yellow caught his attention. His ring was glowing again. It always glowed right at the point of something happening. Blue had meant water was near, white had meant the truth was spoken, gold had been when there was a portal opening to and from Aeliana, black appeared when evil was around, and now the ring was yellow. He wondered if it had to do with wisdom or encouragement.

Ryann yawned, then looked over at his clock. Tomorrow would be a new day, and it would give him a chance to make amends for today. Ryann hoped he had the courage to act out what he had just read about.

As he made his way through the crowded hallway on the way to first period class, Ryann could see the bobbing of Terell's head coming his way.

As they got closer, he noticed Terell veering away from him. "Hey, Terell," he called out.

Terell turned in his direction and Ryann smiled broadly, as he quickened his pace to close the gap between the two.

"Terell," he said again, "I'm really sorry about yesterday."

"That's okay," Terell said, not looking him in the eye.

"No, it's not okay. I was a real jerk yesterday and I need to apologize for how I acted; it wasn't right."

"That's cool," Terell said, a crooked smile nervously trying to form.

"Ya know, Terell, I've never been one to say I'm sorry. I've always just let some time go by and figured everyone would get over it. But now I feel a lot better."

"Now that you mention it, I feel a lot better about it, too. At least we aren't hiding anything from each other. That makes me feel like a closer friend. What made you decide to change?"

Ryann quickly recounted the events of last night with his dad and his word search through Proverbs.

Brrrrrrrrrinnnnnng.

"That Solomon guy was a pretty smart dude," Terell yelled over the bell as they picked up the pace to class.

All was quiet back at the Watters's house. In his dark closet, the third button on Ryann's staff flickered and began glowing white. As much help as it might be in Aeliana, the staff wasn't going to be of any use to him on this day.

CHAPTER 13

Anxious Alleyways

RYANN SPOTTED LYDIA running toward the bike compound. "Where you headed, Liddy?"

"Shopping," she yelled back over her shoulder.

"Girls," Ryann muttered, shaking his head and turning his attention back to Terell.

Something was nagging at her. The previous day had started out normal enough, with Liddy and her mother stopping by her favorite gift shop, Timeless Keepsakes, after school. She was fascinated with the amount of unique items a small store could hold. With the myriad nooks and crannies, colorful mementos, and enduring treasures, the walls bulged forth almost magically to accommodate the increasing numbers of items the friendly shopkeeper had tracked down from all over America. She had planned to purchase something special for Essy, on the chance that she was able to get back to Aeliana. It would have to be small since she would have to have it with her at all times, not knowing if or when her next opportunity would come.

With their new purchases in hand, mother and daughter headed next door for a quick bite at The Windsor Rose, the perfect place to chat among formal English linens and décor, complete with a classic red telephone booth imported from London. After tea they headed over to Donnelly Street to complete the day's shopping at a few of the main street's shops. There was something about the last store of the day that compelled her to return.

Liddy pushed the green wood-framed door open. A small bell jingled overhead as she entered the Madison Rose, a quaint little quilt and gift shop. Adorned with a faded shaker shingle roof, window flower boxes, and dark green and hot pink-trimmed French windows, the shop attracted tourists and locals looking for unique quilts and trinkets. She took a deep breath, savoring the scent of some sort of incense, spicy and sharp, yet strangely pleasant.

She felt drawn to come back to the little store, but she wasn't sure exactly why. It didn't make sense to her. She was used to analyzing things, not making decisions based upon feelings or emotions. Liddy turned to walk back out.

"May I help you with anything?"

Liddy jumped, despite the woman's friendly British accent.

"Oh, I don't think I want anything," she said. "I just came in to look around."

"Really, is that so?" The elderly woman seemed surprised. She looked Liddy up and down, as if wanting to confirm her suspicions. "Okay then, browse around a bit if you like, and let me know if I can be of assistance."

Now Liddy was too embarrassed to walk out. She decided to wander around the store for a few minutes and then slip out when the lady wasn't looking.

Liddy lazily made her way up an aisle of cross-stitch patterns and a wide variety of colored threads. She came to a dead end that had a pile of quilts stacked on top of one another. Liddy knew that a lot of love went into making quilts, but she'd never attempted it and certainly wasn't interested in buying one. As she turned to retrace her steps, a deep purple shape peeked out from under one of the quilts. Reaching over, she lifted the patchwork quilt up and was surprised to find not just a piece, but a rather large amount of cloth folded up neatly into a thick rectangle. Holding the bulky quilts in place, she managed to pull the bolt of fabric out. It felt strangely warm in her hands.

She thought she might be imagining things, yet it felt so comfortable in her hands, like it was meant to be there. Meandering back down the aisle, she came to where the woman had been.

"Where'd you find that, young lady?" the shopkeeper asked, coming out from behind a hanging queen-size quilt.

Liddy jumped for the second time. "Oh, uhh, just at the end of the aisle. I was going to ask you how much it cost."

"Well, it's not for sale, Missy. Here, let me have it."

Liddy handed it over reluctantly and the warm feeling escaped with it. She wanted it more than ever now.

The old woman blinked. A puzzled expression wrinkled across her face. She flipped the cloth over, examining it closely, and then turned her attention back to Liddy, examining her in the same way.

"Do you have fifty cents?" she asked.

"What?"

"I said, do you have fifty cents? You may buy it for fifty cents."

Liddy looked up in surprise. "I thought you said it wasn't for sale."

"It wasn't, but, *it* wants you."

"Checkmate," Ryann proudly announced, as he moved his queen into a forward position, trapping Terell's king.

Terell moaned. "Man, not again."

The last day of school had actually ended early. Liddy didn't feel like it was a good-bye since the three of them had agreed to meet the next morning at Evans Park. Ryann thought she had been strangely preoccupied the past few days, but put it off as he and Terell raced to Dickens-Reed Bookstore to see if anything new was in and play a game of chess.

"Sixth grade is done," Terell concluded.

"Yeah, it seemed to go by so fast. I was hoping that we'd get a chance to go to Aeliana before we all left on summer vacations," Ryann said as he toppled Terell's king.

Ryann surveyed the bookstore they had spent so many hours hanging out in as Terell droned on about his summer plans. There was something about bookstores that fascinated Ryann. Maybe it was the orderliness of the rows and shelves of books or the variety of the size and color of each edition. He had been to the bigger national chain bookstores in Orlando, but there was something special about a locally run store. It had so much more personality and character. Outside, ornate wooden arches framed each window, while the rest of the store facade was composed of carved replicas of various classic books leaning against each other, gargoyles, winding etched vines, and wild carvings that seemed to pop out anew at every visit. Inside, large castle walls with a drawbridge provided the entrance into the children's and teens' area of the store. He had often imagined himself entering a fantasy world as he walked through those gates, and now, ironically enough, he was in his own adventure.

"Yo, Ryann, snap out of it; we need to get going," Terell interrupted.

Ryann jumped up, feeling like he was forgetting something, but today had been the final day of school and they had turned in the last of their books. He took one last look as they exited. He had heard a rumor that the owner, Ruth, was going to have to shut down the store because of the rising cost of rent. He hoped it wasn't true. Change was okay, but not if it put places like this out of business.

The sun hit their eyes as they came out from under the store's eave; at the same time a familiar booming voice erupted.

"Ryann and Terell! Just the two I was looking for," Drake barked.

"Run!" Terell yelled as he bolted to the left.

Ryann didn't have a chance to calm Terell down and remind him that it was two against one, and Drake wouldn't try anything in broad daylight with so many adults around. He quickly decided to confuse Drake by running in the opposite direction as Terell.

As swiftly as he started up Fifth Avenue, Ryann darted right again, down an old brick cobblestone alleyway, known as Dora-Drawdy Way, with Drake in hot pursuit. His mind raced with possibilities for hiding. A fire escape ran up a weathered brick building on his left. If the door was locked at the top he'd be trapped. The end of the same building had bars on the windows and stairs dropping down into a dark alcove. Water dripped off a weathered pipe into the darkness, and Ryann imagined being chained up in a damp, dark dungeon.

Not stopping to look behind him, he raced past The Renaissance, a small mall of stores that housed his mom's favorite flower store, Enchanted Orchids. He considered cutting through there to Donnelly, but Drake might have circled around to the other side. Ryann continued sprinting straight ahead until he came to Fourth Avenue. His heart was pounding in his ears as he stole a glance, whipping his head around to see if Drake was following.

"I'm coming for you, Ryann," Drake yelled as he jogged at a slower pace, confident in being the hunter.

Ryann looked both ways for cars and darted across Fourth Avenue to continue down the cobblestone alleyway. The stately Windsor Rose was on his right, and amidst the anxious escape he was attempting, Ryann briefly pictured Drake chasing him through the formal English tea room, cucumber sandwiches and Earl Grey tea splattering in every direction.

The mixed aroma of the Mount Dora Coffee House and The Goblin Market restaurant's pre-dinner grill hung in the air with an enchanting odor as Ryann's eyes darted about, frantically searching for an escape. With Drake in close pursuit, Ryann decided to take a chance and dove off the cobblestone street just after The Goblin Market. An opening in an old wooden fence led down the informally named Artist Alley. Small one-foot by one-foot cement pavers in double rows wound a little trail through moss-covered water oaks and leftover easels, chairs, and tables from local artists' displays. He navigated through the obstacles with flailing arms, popped out next to The Painter's Daughter on Donnelly Street, and then headed back up the way he had come. "Surely that big idiot won't think I'd go back in the direction I ran from," Ryann hoped.

Unbeknownst to Ryann, his pursuer didn't like the idea of haphazardly cutting between buildings and decided to jog back to Fourth Avenue instead. Just as Ryann was looking to cross Fourth, the hair on the back of his neck shot out.

"Aaahhaaa!"

Drake sounded closer than ever. Ryann never looked back, bolting down Fourth Avenue one block and then turning up another cobblestone alleyway, Royellou Lane. This cut-through was run-down in comparison to the other alleyway, and Ryann hoped the city hadn't cleaned up one of his favorite hiding spots from the past. If only he could make it there without being noticed. Just past a small fading one-story building sat the old city jail that had been turned into a museum. Ryann cut across the gravel parking lot, outlined with bushy trees that shaded the entire area. He skidded to a stop at the back corner of the museum. The roof angled down at the corner, allowing Ryann to step up onto a gutter that was a few feet off the ground, then use a white picket fence that butted up to the building as a ladder. In no time he had scurried like a rat up onto the roof and over behind a vine-covered air conditioner unit.

Every part of his body wanted to betray him. Ryann tried to concentrate in slowing his breathing down, yet his heart was hammering away at the same time. Sweat ran down the small of his back, and he suppressed the desire to reach around and scratch or wipe at it. He needed to stay perfectly still. Glancing down at his watch, Ryann saw that it was five o'clock. His parents would expect him home shortly. His ring had changed to black. Evil was near!

Where was Drake? Why couldn't he see or hear him? Ryann waited. Nothing. He looked at his ring again. The black was replaced with the normal clear glass. Deciding to trust the ring, he made his way across the roof and back down to the parking lot. Slowly Ryann walked along the edge of the gravel parking lot, avoiding empty bottles and old weather-beaten tires—anything that could make noise or cause him to trip. Now what?

"Ryann...I know you're still around here!"

He quickly glanced around and decided to take the route away from Drake's voice. Next to the parking lot a wooden porch fronted a dilapidated two-story brick building. As he leapt onto the porch, it creaked under his weight. Ryann dismissed it, hoping the old boards would hold him. Delicately balancing each footstep, Ryann held out his hands like a trapeze artist. It was then that he noticed the ring abruptly change from clear to red. Ryann froze.

"There you are!" Drake announced.

Ryann glanced over his shoulder to see Drake's shoes throwing up dust as he sprinted across the parking lot to the porch.

Red. What could *red* mean? He didn't have long to make a decision. Ryann looked down at the porch wood in front of him. It was slightly discolored. Maybe red was danger!

Drake was stepping up onto the porch. It was now or never. He stepped over the discolored wood and then sprinted the length of the porch until he could jump off at the end.

Snap!

"Ahhh!"

Ryann turned around to see Drake's feet crashing through the porch flooring he had avoided. Even though Drake was only visible from the waist up, Ryann knew it wouldn't hold him for long. Ryann looked heavenward and smiled, thankful for the warning of the ring.

Ryann glanced at his watch as he waited by the gazebo in Evans Park for Terell and Liddy to show up. As his watch clicked over to nine o'clock, he saw his two closest friends coasting down the hill in front of the park.

"Hey guys," Ryann greeted them at they hopped off their bikes. He noticed the backpack Liddy had slung over her shoulder.

"What's in the backpack, Liddy?"

"Oh, a few presents to say goodbye."

Terell asked. "Cool! For us?"

Liddy rolled her eyes. "Yes, for you guys." She shifted awkwardly, wondering if she had done the right thing. Both of the boys stumbled, leaning forward to see what she was going to pull out of her backpack.

Liddy smiled as she reached into her bag.

"For Terell, I got this!" she announced, pulling out a miniature chrome flashlight.

Terell reached out eagerly. "Wow! Thanks Liddy, this will come in handy with the camping trips and night fishing I do."

Ryann rose up, trying to peer over Liddy's shoulder into the bag. She pulled the bag close to her and said, "Close your eyes and you'll get a big surprise."

Ryann willingly played her game.

"All right, open up."

Ryann's eyes sprang open to see Liddy holding a dark purple shirt out in front of her by the sleeves. It had a unique-looking collar that flared from the top down to a point in the front where the second button on a button-down shirt would have been. The sleeves were cuffed and sewn down with a button on the outside. He wasn't quite sure what to make of it, but grinned quickly.

"Thanks, where did you get it?" Ryann took it from her hands.

"Uhh, I made it myself," she replied sheepishly.

"Really?" the two boys said in unison. Liddy was known for her intellectual prowess and soccer skills, but neither knew that she could sew.

"Yeah, well, my mom taught me how to sew, and I've been trying it out a little."

Ryann didn't know if he would actually wear it. It wasn't that he didn't like it, but it was a little flashier than he normally dressed. Of course, he'd have to wear it around Liddy occasionally so her feelings wouldn't be hurt.

"Try it on, Ryann," Terell said, smiling.

Ryann glared at Terell. He knew that smile. Terell wanted to have a little fun at Ryann's expense and knew there was no way out for him.

"Uhh, yeah, sure," Ryann replied, trying hard not to tip off Liddy that he was none too pleased by the request.

Ryann glanced quickly around the park. At this time in the morning, everything was quiet; even the lake looked like a sheet of glass. "Turn around, while I change shirts."

Peeling his own shirt off wasn't too hard, but the summer humidity made pulling on Liddy's gift very challenging. Carefully he guided his arms through the right holes and then rolled the shirt down his body, trying to smooth it out before they turned around.

"What do you think?" Ryann asked, as his way of saying it was okay to look now.

"It looks great on you," Liddy said. "I like purple."

"Ooh, it's charming," Terell cooed, then backed up quickly as Ryann started to charge at him.

"Boys!" Liddy exclaimed. "I didn't tell you that there's a peculiar story behind my buying the material to make that shirt."

It took a few minutes between the questions, explanations, and retelling of certain details, but Liddy finally got through her encounter at the store and the mysterious answer the woman gave her about the material *wanting* her.

"Do you think she knew something about..." Terell didn't finish the sentence, but instead stared past Ryann and Liddy, mouth still open, but no words coming out.

"Knew something about what, Terell?" Liddy asked.

"Duu...Dra...Drake!" Terell finally yelled.

The other two twirled around to see the dark figure highlighted by the orange flat top, racing down the hill toward them on his bike.

Ryann took charge, surveying the ways of escape around them. "Quick, to the marina," he ordered as the three shot out of the gazebo in a beeline across the dewy St. Augustine grass.

Marina might have been a little formal. That's what it was in its heyday, but that had long since passed. The rickety looking set of open-air buildings, on piling over the water, might still be able to hold their combined weight, but they had seen better days. A mixture of rust and aluminum acted as the roof.

Drake made the transition from the pavement to the grass just as Ryann's foot hit the weathered wooden planks. They groaned under his weight as he raced forward through the deserted marina toward a faded red building in the back.

"Let's hide in the boathouse," Ryann huffed over his shoulder.

Bolting through the space where a door no longer stood, Ryann glanced down at his ring. He was in the habit of checking it since the last time Drake chased him. It was glowing gold!

Ryann made his way briskly toward the back of the boathouse. It was designed in such a way that boats could actually pull into it and then be lifted out by small cranes and stored on either side. The water in the middle of the boathouse was murky in the shadows of the early morning.

"Great, we'll be trapped in here," Liddy gasped, between breaths.

Terell sputtered, "He...he's...sure to have...seen us come in."

Ryann continued looking at the water. "Guys, look at my ring."

"It's gold!" Liddy said excitedly.

"And, it has never been wrong," Ryann added.

The sound of bubbling water tore Liddy and Terell's eyes away from Ryann, and they all watched the familiar, but never tiresome, metamorphosis of the door to Aeliana open up.

"Now it's your turn, Terell," Ryann said confidently.

Liddy smiled happily as the three friends grabbed hands and jumped confidently into the golden circle.

CHAPTER 14

Purple Haze

SOMETHING WAS WRONG, terribly wrong. At first, the travel through the golden portal to Aeliana was normal enough, if you call floating through sparkling goo to another dimension normal. For Ryann it was now routine; even Liddy was calm as she floated weightlessly through the miraculous channel. Watching Terell react to the unique trip made it special for both Ryann and Liddy.

"This is so much more amazing than you even described," Terell's thoughts came across loud and clear to Ryann.

"It sure is, isn't it?" Ryann responded.

Terell looked over at Ryann. His mouth wasn't moving, but he could tell that Ryann was responding to his thoughts. "You can read my thoughts, can't you?" Terell asked.

"Yep," Ryann responded, nodding his head.

Ryann's lips hadn't moved, but Terell heard him all the same, "Cool!"

Everything changed when they burst through into Aeliana. Ryann was looking forward to seeing Terell experience the beauty of this other world, but instead he could only gasp. Where there were once clear skies painted with dozens of blue hues, there was now only a flat, pasty gray. The fruity aroma and tingly wafts of flowery perfume that made his senses jump with excitement on his first visit were replaced with a drab, smoky ash, which caused him to choke when he took his first breath.

Terell's eyes darted about nervously at the mysterious-looking shadows and scraggly trees pressing in around him. "Uhh, guys? I hate to be the one to say it, but this doesn't look like the beautiful place you described to me."

"It isn't, Terell," Ryann answered measurably. "Something is wrong—terribly wrong."

"Here's your staff, Ryann," Liddy cut in. "And look, the third button is lit up."

"That must have happened when I was studying the Bible after getting angry with Terell."

"What do you think it does?"

"We know the first button shoots out a cloud of mist and the second one makes a wall of fire. Stand back and we'll see what happens."

Liddy and Terell took a few steps back behind Ryann as he held the staff out in front of him and slowly squeezed the third button.

Whoosh!

As the swirling white cone burst out of the tip of his staff, Liddy and Terell stepped closer together behind Ryann. The smoke grew wider as it spewed outward and the slight breeze blowing back toward them revealed the secret of the smoke.

"It's cold," Ryann announced as he pointed the staff down at the ground before releasing the button. A patch of icy crystals had formed in the area in front of him.

Terell broke the silence, shivering. "At least we have something to protect ourselves with. I don't like the looks of this place."

"Which direction should we head in?" Liddy looked to Ryann for an answer.

"It's hard to say. It all looks so different, so gray compared to all the colors that should be here." He cocked his head, faintly hearing the rushing sound of cascading water off to their right. "I think Glenys Falls is this way. Come on!"

In one spot, the trees were slightly spread apart and the trio took off in a line, first Ryann, then Liddy, then Terell. Each step brought the dry crunching sound of dead grass, which was so unfamiliar from their previous visits, when lush, flowing green grass shifted gently beneath their feet. The rushing waters grew louder. They were headed in the right direction, but Ryann couldn't shake the feeling that someone was watching them. He held up his hand, signaling Liddy and Terell to stop.

Crunch, crunch. Silence descended upon the trio.

Heads turned in every direction, but they couldn't see anyone. Ryann put a finger to his lips, then waved them forward. They stopped several times over the next hundred yards or so, but the echoing chant of brittle grass never repeated itself.

"Whoa," Ryann cautioned in a whisper, stopping abruptly. Liddy and Terell stumbled into him, but remained quiet.

"Look! Up ahead."

The three of them stood in awe as they entered the shadows of the massive tree. Large oblong-shaped fruit hung down from its branches, some of them a muted pink and some of them black. Ryann recognized the giant trunk of the tree immediately.

"It's the tree of life!" he exclaimed.

Terell wasn't impressed. "Dude, it looks like it's dying to me."

"The tree didn't look this way before. The leaves were so green and the fruit was a bright pink. I think you're right, Terell, but it's not just the tree—Aeliana is dying."

Movement from two dark figures heading their way caught their attention. Ryann decided it would draw too much attention to jump off the path into the scraggly underbrush. And besides, he had the staff. His thumb moved over the third button. He didn't want to be careless and start a forest fire with button two.

The two figures were short and blocky, and both carried swords. They had weathered faces with scruffy black beards and dark circles under their eyes. Ryann thought they were probably hill dwarfs, but he wasn't too good at sorting out the various types of dwarfs at this point. Only the red dwarfs were known to have hot tempers and display unpredictable behavior. They were easy to spot because of their red hair, which never turned gray. These two were obviously comfortable with their surroundings, because they didn't even notice the trio until they were almost upon one another. Then it became eerily quiet. About twenty feet away, the two dwarfs stopped, eyes shifting back and forth between the three figures in front of them, then continued their walk slower toward them. Both of their eyes had settled on Ryann.

"What was up with that?" Ryann asked when they were safely past the two dwarfs.

"With what?" Liddy questioned.

"Come on, don't tell me you didn't notice they were looking at me funny."

Before Liddy or Terell had a chance to respond, the path they had been travelling opened up into a meandering meadow outlining the bowl of water it contained. Ryann knew he had been here before, but it wasn't the same. He did not recall gray, overcast skies in the times he had been to Aeliana. It was those clear blue skies that made the water sparkle so vividly. There was something more. The dryness of the land had affected the lake as well. Where the water ended and the shoreline began, a swath of cracked buckling soil had emerged. The lake was dying. He had been eager to jump into it before. Now the only thing that popped into Ryann's head was split pea soup.

Terell's eyes darted back and forth, settling on Ryann, who was as silent as a statue, staring across the murky lake. "Is something wrong?"

Normally Glenys Falls would have mesmerized anyone. Diamond-like streams of water had cascaded from between rocky cliffs into a clear pool hundreds of feet below, shattering the glassy water on that side of the lake.

Ryann shook his head. "Everything's wrong! Liddy and I were almost in this exact spot on our last visit. It's not supposed to be like this."

Liddy, never one to back away from a challenge, this time deferred to Ryann, "What should we do?"

"We have to continue on to Castle Myraddin and find out what's going on. Maybe we'll run into Raz and Esselyt there or along the way."

"Ooh, I hope so," Liddy said. "I miss her and we had to leave so suddenly last time we were here."

The small band of friends turned together and this time were able to walk side by side as they began making their way around the lake.

As the trio rounded the last bend in the lake, the well-traveled road to Myraddin appeared, and off in the distance the small tip of the highest tower poked its head up. Stepping onto the gravel lane simultaneously pointed them in the direction of oncoming figures of all shapes and sizes.

"Remember, Terell, here in Aeliana, animals can talk and there are a lot of different creatures that we don't have back home, so just act natural," Ryann instructed.

"That's easy for you to say—you've been here before," Terell replied. "I'll do my best, though."

Ryann recalled his last walk along this road as they began the three-mile or so trek; clear blue skies, rolling hills blanketed in glowing emerald grass, wild flowers of various sizes and colors dotting the hillsides. The clashing of the gray sky and pale, sick earth that replaced it caused his stomach to ache. Previously, happy chattering and sing-songy melodies filled the air. Ryann squinted, longing to hear something positive; however, even the air was devoid of life. The first two animals to pass by were a pair of foxes. Ryann nodded in their direction, yet they only stared and continued to trot along.

"Hello," Ryann said in a soft-spoken, yet friendly manner, to a fawn and deer slowly approaching them.

The two nodded respectfully, but didn't speak. Ryann let them pass then turned his head quickly to follow them. Both were staring at him and turned sharply away at being caught. After several more episodes of the same behavior with elves, several types of cats, and horses, Liddy was first to bring up the issue.

"You do realize, Ryann, that everyone is staring at you."

"Me? Why me?"

"I don't know, but there's something about you that's making them act funny—like they don't know what to say or how to react to you. Is there anything different about you from the last time you were here?"

He glanced at himself as they continued the pace. "No, not that I can tell. Yet another question to ask when we get to the castle."

Ryann became more self-conscious of the stares and silent treatment he was getting from creatures that passed him as Myradinn loomed larger and larger in front of them. Previously, Ryann had seen the castle as a miraculous wonder of engineering, with its massive stone walls, soaring towers, and sculpted masonry around the doors and windows. Now lifeless and dark, the former liveliness had been squeezed out, exposing an empty, dank husk. Passing through the yawning mouth of the ancient stone archway that led into the courtyard of the castle, Ryann's eyes were drawn to the purple banner ordained with an ornate gold W, hanging down from the arch midpoint. It wasn't so long ago that they were bowing in reverence to the penetrating light when the three blue moons had come together as one.

"Essy!" Liddy cried out. "Are you there?" Her voice echoed eerily into the dark tunnel.

They waited a few seconds for a response.

"Raz!" Ryann bellowed.

Echoes bounced off the walls again.

The three huddled together. "Should we just stroll in?" Liddy asked.

Ryann waited silently with his eyes shut and his lips barely moving. Liddy knew he was praying.

The pitter-patter, pitter-patter of someone approaching alerted the group they were soon to have company. The soft steps bounced off the old walls, followed by chattering noises, until one could be distinctly heard, "I'm telling you, I heard Ryann. I recognize the voice and—"

Ryann had a silly grin on his face as Raz and Essy popped out of the shadows.

Maintaining his stately poise, Raz held out a paw, "Ryann, my boy, it's a pleasure to see you again." Essy on the other hand was up on her hind legs, giving Liddy an awkward hug of sorts. "Essy, I'm so glad to be back in Aeliana," Liddy mused as she returned the leopard's hug. Raz noticed the fidgeting boy behind them and cut the happy reunion short.

"Ryann, aren't you going to introduce your travelling companion?"

"Travelling who? Oh, yeah, Terell. I'm sorry. Raz and Essy, this is Terell."

"It's a pleasure to meet you, Terell. Any friend of Ryann's is a friend of ours," Raz said, extending his hairy paw.

Terell slowly reached out to shake the raccoon's paw, mesmerized by his first opportunity to meet a talking animal. "Th...thanks."

With the pleasantries out of the way, Raz had a few questions. "Ryann, where did you get that shirt?"

"What, this?" He asked pinching the loose-fitting garment. "From Liddy. She made it for me."

"Interesting," Raz squinted while nodding knowingly.

"What, Raz?" Liddy asked as she crossed her arms.

Essy came to her defense. "He's not making a judgment about your seamstress abilities, Liddy, it's the color. It's purple."

"And what's wrong with purple?"

Essy nodded to Raz, who continued, "Nothing is wrong with the color. It's just that in Aeliana, purple is a sign of royalty. The only people who wear it are considered to be working directly for the Word."

"Ahh, that would explain all of the stares and nods I received while we were walking here," Ryann bellowed, thrusting his hands in the air.

"But what about the skies and the land?" Liddy asked. "Everything was so beautiful the last time we were here."

"Dreadful, just dreadful," Raz shook his head. "At first there were odd patches of gray-black, scorched earth, popping up throughout the kingdom. Then rumors began spreading that some of the citizens of Aeliana were no longer following the Word and that they had found someone else to follow."

"Drake!" Ryann shouted.

"What?" Essy asked.

"Not what, who. Drake has to be responsible for this."

"How can you say that, Ryann?" Liddy asked. "I know he's mean and all, but he doesn't even have a way to get here."

"I don't know how I know. I just feel it," Ryann responded.

"Well, regardless of who," Raz continued, "it is apparent that there may be some truth to the rumor of another leader challenging the teaching of the Word. I believe that is what is causing the skies to darken and the earth to dry up."

Essy added, "No one knows what to do."

"Raz, remember my purpose in coming to Aeliana was to find the sword that the angel Gabriel had sent me to look for?"

"How could I forget?"

"I found an important clue as to its location, and I can't believe that what is happening here in Aeliana is a coincidence. I need to find that sword!"

"Mmmm. I believe you're right, young Ryann." Raz rubbed his chin. "We must escort you to the High Council immediately and get their insight."

"Where is that?"

Raz looked back into the darkness they had come out of. "In there."

CHAPTER 15

River
Quest

AKING THEIR WAY through the stone corridors that extended in a bevy of disjointed directions and doorways made it difficult to know their exact location. Passing through a cavernous room with massive timbers crisscrossing the arched ceilings, Liddy recalled with remarkable clarity the evening in which they feasted before the Word spoke. Magnificent stained-glass windows with a kaleidoscope of colorful rays pouring through to illuminate the special dining area had been snuffed out, and joyful banquet laughter and talking were now distant echoes. Empty chairs covered in a fine layer of dust outlined the lengthy dining room table that was starving for another meal.

Raz and Essy, who were leading the way, slowed as they came to two massive wooden doors. Creatures of all shapes and sizes—dragons in battle, galloping unicorns, roaring lions, and soaring eagles—were intricately carved into the smooth, tanned wood. Unlike the rest of the dingy walls, the doors were polished into a wet glaze. Three blue moons adorned the peak of the entryway, shining down on the created beings. Essy stood up on her hind legs and lifted the rung of one of the heavy brass knockers.

Boom!

They waited, listening to the echoes die down. Raz and Essy, with their ears pointed up, were alert yet otherwise calm. Ryann glanced over to catch Terell nibbling on his fingernails. The massive doors shook as they were initially opened, then began creaking as they widened to let them in. Raz went through first. Essy waved Ryann, Liddy, and Terell through next, then briefly scanned behind them before following.

Dark blue marble floors paved the way into the room. Highly polished like the entry doors, they reflected what little light there was, like a pond on a still day. Seven smooth, round, white pillars, encased at the top and bottom by thick square blocks of the same white stone, lined both sides of the room. At the far reaches of the room, seven stairs led up to a platform that held seven golden chairs. The padding on the seat and back of each chair was covered in purple velvet. On the chairs sat the seven members of the High Council.

Making their way in hesitant strides up to the council, they stopped just short of the purple carpet, with the same golden W sewn into it. Raz and Essy were out front and bowed slightly. Lined up in a row behind them, the children nodded to imitate their animal companions, and then looked up to observe the figures in front of them. A variety of animals and humanoids faced them: a pointy-eared elf, black bear, zebra, dwarf, red fox, a human man and woman, and the central figure towering over the rest. His face was weathered and adorned with a long, white beard. Kind gray eyes twinkled back at them. His flowing white robes added a scant thickness to his gaunt appearance.

Raz addressed the white-bearded man with the flowing-white robes bunched up on the floor beneath him. "Chancellor Aodan, we come before you today with a matter of great urgency. If you will permit, I will try to be brief in my summary of my experience with the three travelers who are with us today."

Ryann observed the faces of the council members for any indication of what they may be thinking as Raz summarized their first encounter through today. Fortunately, raccoons are second only to squirrels in their chattering ability, and Raz was able to finish in less than thirty minutes. He bowed politely again at the conclusion, folded his paws in front of himself, and waited.

Chancellor Aodan stared at each of them individually for several minutes, as if peering into their souls to determine who they were. Ryann was certain his body was warming as the pale-skinned sage gazed into his eyes. He just wasn't sure if it was his nerves or his inner feelings being revealed to the high councilman.

When Chancellor Aodan finally spoke, his deep voice was smooth and reassuring. "There is no such thing as coincidence; therefore, the purple cloth of Ryann speaks of the truth of the quest he has been given. I have only one question."

Everything around Ryann faded away from his vision. It was as if the elder statesman and he were the only two people in the room. "Our world is being attacked by the evil one. The great deceiver's grip has tightened around those who desire fanciful things and fleeting pleasures. They believe his lies and have accepted the temporal over that which is everlasting." He completed his observations and stared at him more intently, "Ryann?"

Ryann was unsure as how to address him. "Yes, sir?"

"What is truth?"

The question caught him off-guard. "What is truth?" Ryann repeated the question to himself. Of all of the questions he could have been asked, surely the sage would have rather chosen, Where do you think the sword is? Or, How do you think we can help you? His eyes narrowed as he considered whether it was a trick question. Ryann knew that some people say truth is whatever you believe to be true. Yet that didn't seem right, because what if you believe something is true and someone else doesn't? How could you both be right? He had heard someone say, "What's true for you might not be true for me." But he wondered, "Shouldn't real truth be true for everyone whether they choose to believe it or not?"

Ryann's head began to ache. What is truth? He didn't know how long he had to answer, but he knew it was important that he gave the right answer. He pictured himself sitting in his room at home reading his Bible. The Bible was God's Word. He had been pouring over it day and night in search of answers to the whereabouts of the sword. In his mind, Ryann opened the Bible, picturing the book of John at the end of chapter 3 and he tried to translate it as those in Aeliana would hear it. Clearing his throat, he responded, "Whoever believes in the Word has eternal life, but whoever rejects the Word will not see life."

All eyes focused on the wise old man as he breathed in Ryann's answer, closed his eyes for a brief moment, then opened them and replied: "You have answered wisely."

Ryann exhaled, relieved.

"Please leave us for a moment as we determine the next course of action," the High Council ordered.

Waiting in silence outside in the hall was too much for Ryann, as he finally blurted out a question to Raz. "What do you think they're going to do?"

"My experience with the council is that they seek wisdom from the Word, consider the resources they have available, and then provide clear directions. The council members are our most revered citizens, ordained by the Word to provide leadership on a daily basis."

"I like it. They sound like a logical and sensible group," Liddy said.

"You would," Terell said shaking his head, "—structure and logic."

Ryann continued the questioning. "Once they give us their decision, do we have to go along with it?"

Essy's one eyebrow rose and her brow wrinkled, "It would be unheard of not to follow their direction."

"Essy is correct. Let us wait and see the outcome before thinking such thoughts," Raz said just before silence pressed in on them again while they sat thinking about what was to come.

Bong!

Ryann looked over at Raz upon hearing the loud noise through the thick entry door into the council chamber.

"They have made their decision. We will be ushered back in shortly."

Moments later the oak door pushed open, and the small group was led to their previous positions for Aodan to reveal the council's decision.

"We have come to the conclusion that your party must leave at once to seek out the King's sword. It is part of the answer to the evil that has entered our world."

"Yes, Chancellor." Raz bowed. "We will leave at once." Before they could turn to leave, Aodan cleared his throat and continued.

"And Griffin will go with you," he added, pointing in the direction of the dignified-looking red fox sitting to his right.

Leaping off the stage with grace and confidence, the fox landed in front of the small group. He spoke clearly and directly to them. "We must leave at once."

"Cast off!" grunted the boar, waddling alongside their boat on the stone pier.

Raz gripped the rope in his mouth and violently thrust his head up, flinging the rope away to separate them from the dock at Castle Myraddin. It had been Griffin's idea to take the Pedr River east, which would carry them directly between the Joynnted Knolls and Marrow Mountains. Essy had not been keen to the idea. Like all cats, she had a dislike of water and wasn't quite sure she could swim if she had to. Ryann thought it was a brilliant way to both expedite the speed of their travel and minimize the effort walking required.

Simplicity was at the core of the boat's design. Stretching out about six feet across and twenty feet long, the basic wooden shell would suffice for their needs. Six crewmembers were more than enough to maneuver it through the waters: a lookout at the bow, two each amidships, and someone to direct the tiller. Ryann had at first wondered about how it would be powered, but due to the natural water flow from the falls it wasn't necessary to have a sail. Steering through the river's current and avoiding rocks or shallow water would be the primary focus.

Griffin sat up on his haunches at the bow of the vessel. A rust-red coat of fur, highlighted by a white patch on his chest, created a regal image. Everything seemed perfect about the fox, until Ryann's eyes drifted down to his tail. His red fur changed to white as the tail fluffed outward, however the last several inches were bluntly chopped off. Ryann approached him, imaging a ferocious battle in which the fox had saved someone at a bloody expense. Alone on the bow, Ryann decided not to ask about Griffin's tail, as he looked out over the river they were drifting down. Liddy and Essy were staring vacantly over the sides while Terell and Raz sat on the stern peering back at where they had come from.

"Griffin, sir?" Ryann said, breaking the silence.

"Griffin would be just fine, thank you."

"How long will we continue on this river?"

"It depends on which direction we decide to take."

"Direction?"

"Yes," Griffin answered. "In a few hours we will have to choose whether to continue on the Pedr River, which heads south toward the Marrow Mountains; on the Elan River, which continues east into the desert; or up the Bryn River, which heads north into the Joynnted Knolls."

"Which way do you think we should we go?"

"Your choice in which course we take and how you determine it is important, young adventurer. It is not my decision to make. I am but a part of your quest."

Ryann retreated to a corner of the boat where he could be alone. Leaning over the side, he watched the murky water rushing past and tried to recall the verse he had read a few nights ago, "It penetrates even to dividing soul and spirit, joints and marrow; it judges the thoughts and intentions of the heart." He knew that the "joints and marrow" was referring to the Joynnted Knolls and Marrow Mountains, so the sword would be somewhere between the two, but which river should they take? With three choices, there was a chance he would guess correctly. Liddy would tell him to gather all the facts and then try to make the most intelligent decision. Ryann considered the two options and decided upon a third. He dropped to his knees and closed his eyes to pray.

"Has the water always been this dirty?" Liddy asked Essy as they chatted amidships across from Ryann. Terell and Raz piloted the boat with a wooden tiller, from the stern.

"Certainly not," Essy said. "Up until a few days ago, all the waters of Aeliana were so clean you could see clear to the bottom."

"Is this the first time that some sort of evil has inhabited your land?"

"I have never seen anything like this," Essy replied. "Nor have any of my kind passed down stories of anything like this happening in the past."

Liddy glanced over her shoulder and saw Ryann on his knees. "I sure hope he knows what he's doing," she whispered to Essy.

Ryann recalled the voice of the Word from the first time they were in Castle Myraddin, "If you will treasure my commandments within you...cry out for discernment...then you will discover the fear of the Word and discover My knowledge." Ryann knew that the commands came from the Bible, and he had spent the past weeks pouring over the Scriptures, both reading and meditating on them.

Opening his eyes, Ryann looked around; everyone was looking at him. Before he had been visited by Gabriel, he would have been embarrassed at his actions. But his view on what was normal and what was right had changed. Now his hope was in the Word. "Uhh, did I just yell out?"

He looked around at the nodding heads. Then it came to him.

"I've been thinking, actually praying, about which river I should choose," Ryann began. He continued to survey their faces and could see each of them leaning forward to hear what he was going to say next. "I was reminded of some wisdom from the Word. He said, 'In our hearts we plan our course, but the Word determines our steps.'" Again, they inched closer for his next statement.

"That's it," Ryann finished, watching each bewildered onlooker's face scrunch up quizzically, all except for the fox, who nodded in agreement, eyes sparkling.

Dreadful screams filled the air, breaking the brief silence. Turning away from Ryann and looking toward the banks of the river on each side, bushes shook with the trampling boots of dark figures as they rustled along the shoreline.

"Stay low!" Griffin shouted.

Up ahead the brush thinned to bare sand on the north side. Empty and motionless, it would be easy to see if anything alive entered it. On the south side of the river stood an array of creatures dressed in black with flying red dragons painted on the front. There were several dozen dwarfs, hobgoblins, and trolls, with a few black bears, a panther, and gray wolves all baring their teeth. Their leader stood in front of them—Drake Dunfellow.

"Ryann! Give up and I vow that no harm will come to your pathetic little group," Drake shouted.

"Wh...wha...what's he doing here?" Terell spat out.

Ryann clenched his teeth as everyone on the boat looked to him for a response. The hair on the nape of Essy's neck was standing on end.

Glaring at his adversary, Ryann thought about Drake's bully tactics back home, but here he had changed. He had become meaner and appeared to be many years older than thirteen. Dark circles gathered under his black and lifeless eyes. The true nastiness of his inner character had boiled to the surface here in Aeliana. Ryann's anger flared, but there was also an odd mixture of feeling sorry for him.

"Time's up, Ryann. What's it going to be?" Drake asked.

Ryann's eyes were drawn downward to the dragon, poised for battle, on Drake's chest. He pushed his own nervousness aside and allowed himself to be filled with the confidence of the Word. "No, Drake, you may have numbers on your side, but the Word is on our side and will deliver us today!"

Drake's eyes briefly flashed red and he barked. "Archers, raise your bows!"

Ryann didn't wait for his next command. Pointing his staff in the direction of the dark hoard, he pressed button one.

Phsssssst!

Misty rain shot out of the tip, expanding into a huge cloud, blocking the enemy from seeing them. Yells from the surprised attackers floated up from the other side. Continuing to drift down the river, Ryann kept the cloud between them and Drake's small army until the cries grew faint and he could release his thumb. Cheers rang out from Terell, Liddy, and their animal friends. Ryann shrugged his shoulders as a silly grin spread across his face.

"Well done," Griffin said.

Raz couldn't help but add, "Very impressive, Ryann."

"Oh, and by the way," Griffin continued to the group, "in the excitement of the encounter, our choice was made for us."

"What choice?" asked Terell.

"Which river to head down. We missed the Bryn and Pedr offshoots and have continued into the Elan River."

"Oh no," bemoaned Terell. "You mean we can't go back and choose one of the other routes?"

"I'm comfortable with the direction," Liddy said. "I'm not sure what Bryn and Pedr mean, but the name *Elan* means 'life' and that sounds good enough for me."

Terell cracked, "Man, she would know that."

Ryann jumped back into the conversation, "It's okay. I prayed about it. I believe the Word has answered me by directing our steps, or in this case our boat, this way."

"How did Drake end up getting into Aeliana?" Terell asked.

"The only logical answer is that he jumped into the gold circle after us, before it closed up," Liddy quipped.

"This girl doesn't ever stop," Terell laughed.

Over the next few hours, the shoreline scenery changed as they floated along. Overgrown brush along the south bank of the river and large shade trees thinned out to the same barren surface as the north bank. Griffin maintained his lookout on the bow. They split up on either side of the boat to keep a watch for any more ambushes, Liddy and Essy on one side and Ryann and Terell on the other. Raz kept a steady paw on the tiller to keep them centered on the waterway.

"Did you notice it's getting a lot warmer?" Terell asked.

"We are headed into the barren desert, ya know," Ryann answered. "I would expect it to get a lot hotter than this."

"How are we gonna know when to get off the boat?" Terell asked, ignoring his friend's bluntness.

"Griffin said there would be no question as to when we would get off."

"Ahh, I see, just like it's obvious that it should be getting warmer because we're headed into a desert," Terell said, directing his attention back to his lookout duties.

Ryann winced, hoping that tempers wouldn't start to get the better of them with the heat and new dangers they were experiencing.

Drifting along for another hour or so, with the sun directly overhead and no shade on the open-air boat, excess movement became tiring, so they drifted in silence. On both banks of the river and as far as they could see, there was only sand. Ryann thought it odd that the river did not dry up in the desert. He glanced down into it again and was surprised to see it had become so clear that he could see the mixed sand and rock bottom.

"This is the end of the boat ride," Griffin announced abruptly. "Raz, steer us to the left bank."

Staggering to their feet, they held tightly to the sides for balance as the boat lurched toward shore. Ryann slowly made his way forward to the bow, where Griffin stood. It certainly was obvious. An opening, no higher than two feet above the surface, was covered over in a mound of rocks. The river flowed into the small opening so that there was no way to continue by boat, or swimming for that matter.

Raz masterfully guided the boat to a soft landing on the north shore as the weary travelers began putting together the few supplies they had brought with them. There would be enough dried food for three days, a utility knife, and canteens.

"Fill up your canteens; we don't know where the next source of water will be," Griffin directed. It was a quick exercise done in silence to conserve energy. Getting off the boat had brought them to life, but the sun was working its best to sap their strength.

"Now, Ryann, which way?" the red fox asked.

CHAPTER 16

Desert of Darkness

RYANN LOOKED NORTH, then east, then south. There was sand in every direction. Not the mountainous hills of sand he had seen on television or in the movies, but smaller rolling slopes of sandy earth for as far as he could see. The last thing he wanted to do was discourage anyone in the group, but he really had no idea which direction to go. He was fairly certain they should not retrace the direction they had come from, so once again it left him with three options.

"Ryann, perhaps this would help," Griffin said, extending his paw, which was holding a small, wooden cylindrical object. Ryann took it from the fox and quickly examined the glass at both ends.

"A binoc...err...monocular?"

"Something like that," Griffin replied, "It should lengthen your line of sight."

Ryann put the portable wooden telescope, which was designed for someone the size of a fox, up to his right eye and peered through it. The sandy hills extended further out than before. Looking to the north, way off in the distance he could make out the Joynnted Knolls peaking over the rolling sandy plains. Slowly he began rotating to the right. Peering almost directly east, a mound of rocky formations jutted out of the sand. Ryann lowered the monocular slightly and peered over the top. With his naked eye, the formations couldn't be seen. Looking through it again, the jagged formations returned. Continuing his scan of the horizon, he moved south until he could see the Marrow Mountains far off in the distance.

"We head east," Ryann announced.

There were no arguments after what they had experienced during their encounter with Drake and his hoard of followers. Picking up their gear, they left the boat and headed up the small embankment into the barren desert.

"Essy, I do hope we're going to find the sword out here," Liddy half-stated, half-asked, as they matched up in pairs. Moving out in three small groups, Ryann and Griffin led from the front. Essy and Liddy followed about twenty feet behind with Terell and Raz following roughly the same distance after them.

Essy purred softly.

"What?" Liddy asked.

"Well, Liddy, when you say *hope* you make it seem like chance or a wish," Essy answered quietly.

"Isn't that what hope is?"

"Let me explain it this way," Essy continued. "For us, our faith in the Word is looking back and seeing what He has done. Our hope then, for the future, is based on our confidence in this faith."

Liddy processed what she had just heard. "So, you're saying that your hope for the future isn't based on blind faith, but on actual experience of what you've seen the Word do for you in the past?"

Prrrrr...

Footprints of each human and animal pair clearly marked their path as they determinedly made their way into the desert. Terell looked back occasionally and thought how odd it would seem to someone back home viewing the footprints of a leopard, raccoon, and fox alongside three people. The terrain was the same rippling sandy hills as far as they could see in every direction. From Ryann's scouting background, he had confirmed with Griffin that the sun rose in the east and set in the west, just like back home. Ryann observed their shadows beginning to grow as the sun passed overhead and continued blazing behind them; only now, the shadows were disappearing. Both he and Griffin looked over their shoulders at the same time. Six figures gasped, in their own unique ways, as an ash-gray sediment rose along the western skyline, instantly muddying the cloudless blue sky.

Terell sputtered, "I...is it a...a...sandstorm?"

No one responded as they watched the sky continue to darken, like the night rising from west to east, until the sun was barely visible behind it. Looking to one another for answers, they could see it wasn't dark like nighttime because they were all clearly visible to one another, but it was more than just an instantaneous overcast sky. The effectiveness of the sun's rays was limited to a white circle clearly outlined behind a sheet of ashy-gray darkness.

"Griffin, has this ever happened in Aeliana before?" Ryann asked.

"Not in my lifetime."

Liddy spoke up. "It has to be Drake's doing."

Ryann quickly looked at his ring. It was black.

"Stay close together and let's move up to the top of this next hill," Ryann said, motioning them forward with a wave of his hand. Griffin and he reached the crest first and peered over the top. Shadowy figures were moving slowly in a long line. He gestured for everyone to lie down.

"Who are they?" Ryann whispered to Griffin.

"Mmmm. I can only assume they are part of the same group we left behind on the river."

"Ryann, there's some movement to our right," Liddy cried softly up to them.

He scanned to the south. A line of dark cloaked figures had emerged over the distant rise and was headed toward them. Ryann felt his muscles tighten.

"They know," Griffin said. "They know we're here!"

"Then we retreat at once," Ryann answered. "We can outrun them and get back to the boat."

"Ryann, behind!"

The voice came from Raz at the back of their group. Ryann whipped around. Another line of cloaked figures, a hundred at least, was just now emerging over the dunes to the west, between them and the river.

It was a trap.

Ryann plunged down the hill. "To the north, hurry!"

The group between them and the boat came into clear view now, a long line that stretched farther than he first thought. While they had been watching the group out front, the remaining horde had circled behind. Or worse, more were on the way.

They were now flanked on the east, west, and south. Surely Drake knew that they would simply run north out of the trap.

Unless...

He saw the dark figures ahead, coming from the direction of the Joynnted Knolls. But how many? Too many to count, cutting off their escape.

"Back!"

They retreated up toward their original position. There was no sense running blindly. He would survey the situation from the highest elevation to determine their next course of action. Atop the dune, their predicament became abundantly clear. Drake's army lumbered toward them from every direction. Their movement was slow and methodical, as if they wanted them to realize the hopelessness of their situation. Ryann looked for a break in their ranks, but each time he saw one, it closed.

They had been outwitted by Drake.

Ryann considered his options. They were completely surrounded. Peering through the monocular, he quickly made a panoramic scan to determine where the enemy was weakest. Directly to the east, in the direction they had been heading, the shadowy figures were spaced apart at greater distances. Just above the enemies' heads, Ryann could make out the piles of boulders he had seen earlier, which first led him to head in an easterly direction. Beyond the boulders the ground split open into a ravine.

"Gather 'round," Ryann said, motioning to the group. "Here's the plan."

Hastily conceived in the few seconds he had looked over the enemy and terrain, Ryann pushed aside any doubts trying to force their way in. Through the monocular, he had been viewing the rolling dunes as an unexpected vision flashed before his eyes, revealing their escape route.

"Do you really think that will work?" Liddy asked.

Terell came to his friend's defense. "We don't have much time or many options, Liddy, and besides, Ryann got us out of the last jam, didn't he?"

Liddy's silence confirmed Terell's point.

Ryann jumped out in front, and Liddy and Essy moved into position behind him, followed by Terell and Raz. Griffin took up the final spot at the rear. Bunching up as close as possible, they all looked toward Ryann and waited for his signal.

Ryann looked left, then right. The enemy, on both sides, was still a little way off. Behind them the bobbing of black hoods was just coming into view. By his estimation, it would be another few minutes before they would be spotted. Focusing his attention in front of them again, Ryann no longer needed the monocular to see the menacing faces approaching them.

Black shoals draped over creatures of varying shapes and sizes announced the oncoming evil. Dark, faceless holes in the hoods kept them from seeing exactly who their enemy was. A few had fury snouts sticking out, and one hood with a grotesque albino nose, swollen with marble-sized bumps and red sores, made him turn his head away in disgust.

Hidden just over the rise, they wouldn't be visible to the enemy in front of them until they were stumbled upon. Ryann recalled the battles of Joshua in the Bible. They were always outnumbered, but they typically had the element of surprise. "The enemy will never suspect us to take the fight to them," Ryann thought.

"Just a few more steps," Ryann whispered to himself.

"*Now!*"

All six sprang up as one, charging over the rise and down the hill toward the forty black hoods at the bottom. In the few seconds it took for the cloaked creatures to realize what was happening, Ryann pointed his staff at the ground out in front of them and pushed button three.

Whoosh!

Frosty air shot out of the staff in a white stream, spreading a sheet of ice in front of them.

"Jump!" Ryann yelled above the shouts of the confused enemy.

Hurling themselves forward in unison, the six landed onto the icy ground. Ryann's thumb turned white holding the button down forcefully, while focusing on spraying the ground out in front of them. Dark figures dodged and jumped to the side to avoid the tumbling and flopping group sliding down the hill past them.

"Get them, you cowards!" one of the larger hooded creatures barked, "or you will answer to Lord Ekron."

If not for the perilous danger they were in, Ryann and his friends would have been laughing on the ice slide he had created as they slid down the makeshift toboggan run. Slowing at the start of the next hill, he took his finger off the button. Tumbling off the ice, they skidded into the dirt. With a frenzied pace they scrambled to an upright position.

"Run for the rocks!" Ryann yelled.

Ignoring the shouts, howls, and growls behind them, Ryann, Liddy, and Terell sprinted toward the huge boulders that rested one hundred or so yards out in front of them. Raz raced out ahead to scout what they were heading into. Essy and Griffin turned to face the hoard, snarling and baring their teeth, trying to keep the black cloaks off guard.

Raz met the trio as they dodged behind the first large boulder.

"Down this path, quickly!" he motioned frantically with his black paw.

"You lead them down, Raz, and wait for the rest of us," Ryann countered. "I'll hold them off with the staff until Essy and Griffin are safe!"

Raz didn't argue, scurrying down a small, winding pathway that led into the shadows below. Terell and Liddy stumbled after him, sliding on the pebbles and other loose debris on the path. Scraggly brush lined the trail along the steep decent, and Raz wondered if they'd find a place to hide in the barren ravine.

Ryann whirled about, peering around the side of the jagged rock. Essy and Griffin were racing toward him, eyes wide open, their hind legs kicking up sand with every thrust forward. Animal expressions were hard for him to read, but there was no doubt that fear was flashing out of their eyes. They were only twenty-five yards away, but Ryann's attention was on the hundreds of black cloaks forming a sea of darkness on the horizon behind them. Arrows lit with fire streamed through the air to the left and behind the leopard and fox as they dodged around the boulder.

"Run down the path!" Ryann shouted. "Everyone else is below. I'll follow you in just a second." Essy and Griffin scattered down the same skinny path. Again Ryann turned to face the enemy, his ring glowing the same ominous blackness as the hoard. "If they want fire, I'll give them fire," Ryann muttered to himself.

With Essy and Griffin safely behind the boulders, the hail of fire arrows had stopped. As the gray skies darkened and the wind began to pick up, the advancing dark cloaks created waves of rolling blackness. Confident with their superior numbers, the advancing army moved ahead toward the boulders Ryann was hiding behind. Waiting until they were just outside the reach of the flames, he jabbed the staff forward and pushed button two.

Swoooooosh!

Swirling fire jetted out of the staff's tip, building a wall of flames between them. The blazing fire erupted skyward and extended fifty feet on either side of him, repelling the darkness. Cries from the faceless enemy filled the nighttime air. Numerous shrouds burst into flames, the victims diving to the ground, rolling to put them out in the sand.

Ryann focused so intently on the veiled enemy regrouping in small dark pockets outside the reaches of the flaming wall that he didn't notice the larger shadow looming above. Gliding effortlessly down toward the crackling firewall, Ryann had a brief moment to glance up at the great winged creature swooping in. Outstretched black wings flared out from the back of a muscular man-like creature. Ryann's eyes were drawn to the intensely handsome face with the piercing black eyes. With a quick clapping motion of his wings, Ryann's fiery wall collapsed into a flickering candle-like flame. Darkness pressed in on him and Ryann's skin began to crawl with goosebumps from the unusually cool air. Towering at least seven feet tall, the frightening, yet princely, black angel faced Ryann from fifty feet away. His stare pierced into Ryann's soul, as his mouth widened into a twisted smile. Ryann tried to look away, but the hypnotizing glare froze him in place. His feet wouldn't do what his brain was commanding—run. Ryann's insides churned, both hands clenching tightly to suppress his fear. As the twisted smile grew,

Ryann focused on a small thin scar he hadn't noticed at first on the beautiful face. Starting at the top of his forehead, the pink line ran jaggedly down along the side of his face. Ryann shook his head, the imperfection bringing him out of his trance.

"Now, Ryann Watters, I am going to teach you a little lesson in good versus evil. Let's match the powers of Lord Ekron against, oh, I'm sorry, where is your little angel, Gabriel?"

Lord Ekron began to laugh. He laughed so hard that the surrounding dunes rang with it, as though a dozen Ekrons were laughing at once.

Ryann was thinking fast, weighing his chances. He was no match for this demon, but he had bought his friends time to get farther away. Ryann noticed movement from behind Lord Ekron.

The demon turned, "Oh, allow me to introduce my apprentice. Ahhh, but I see you've already met!" His crooked smile returned as Drake Dunfellow stepped from the shadows.

CHAPTER 17

Straining Ahead

RYANN TRIED TO suppress a shocked look. He didn't want to fuel their laughter. And where was Gabriel? Drake had Lord Ekron at his side—or it was more like Lord Ekron had Drake—but he had no one.

Drake mimicked the confidence of his master with glee. "Don't think I haven't forgotten about you shoving me in class, Ryann. Now, where's the sword?"

Ryann's flickering staff was the only illumination in the surrounding area. Ryann knew he had to act quickly while he still had a few options. Releasing his finger, the flame extinguished itself, and in the brief total blackness, Ryann dove behind the boulder. Within seconds, raspy flames spewed from Lord Ekron's mouth. "Get him!" he breathed in a snarl of bellowing fire.

Ryann ran in the direction of the narrow pathway where the others had descended. He winced and then pushed down gently on button two. Sputtering back to life, the small flame produced enough light for him to see. Rushing forward, he stumbled and slid down the path, willing himself to stay upright until he reached the bottom. His tiny yellow-orange flame cast a dilapidated glow across the rocky canyon floor.

"Hello?" he cried out softly, lifting his finger off the button so they wouldn't see him from above.

"There's no way out, Ryann!" Drake yelled from above, his echoes carrying down the canyon walls. "My army will surround you and at first light it will all be over."

"*Psssst*, over here."

Ryann lit his staff again, convinced from Drake's comments that they wouldn't be coming after them tonight. Waving it in a circle around him raised a soft glow, revealing five sets of eyes returning his stare. "Man, are we glad to see you," Terell said, coming out from among the shadows. "What happened up there?"

Moving out of the open, under the overhang of the cliffs, Ryann sat down and gave a detailed description of his encounter with Lord Ekron and Drake.

"I just knew Drake was part of this," Liddy acknowledged. "But have you heard of this Lord Ekron?" she asked turning to Griffin, Essy, and Raz.

"This is new to us," Raz replied. "There has never been anyone to rebel against the Word. Griffin?"

"We had once heard a rumor that one of the mightiest beings created by the Word had turned his back on Him and then had been banished with other rebels to a distant land. But nothing has ever come of it—until now."

"Well, whoever Lord Ekron is, he squelched the fire on the staff Gabriel gave me. I don't know how much use it will be against him. Any other ideas?" Ryann asked.

"I have the horn you gave me to carry," Liddy announced.

"Do we really even know what it does?" Ryann asked to no one in particular.

Raz quickly answered. "It caused fear and trembling to Essy and me when you blew one long blast at the tree of life."

"They seem to thrive on fear. Somehow I don't see that as a solution." Ryann countered. "Any other ideas?"

Heavy sighs of frustration and angst filled the air as urgency for an answer eluded them. Terell broke the silence. "Hey! Didn't we read a story in Sunday school once about Moses and his men blowing their horns for the walls of the city of Jericho to come down?"

"That was Joshua, but what's the point?" Liddy responded sharply. "I don't see any city walls."

"Come now, come now, we can't have division among ourselves. We need to keep our wits about us," Raz counseled.

"Mmm. There's something about what Terell said that's intriguing to me. Something I'm missing," Ryann pondered loud enough for them all to hear.

"Look out!" Liddy screamed.

In an instant, Ryann saw the fiery arrow blazing through the black sky. Their slow leg muscles tensed, paralyzing them from diving out of the way. It was too late. Whizzing through the middle of them, the arrow struck Griffin in the side.

Thump!

"Where did it come from?"

"Quick, run after him!"

Everyone was shouting. Essy sprinted in the direction she thought the arrow came from. In the confusion, no one noticed the cloak of darkness that Drake threw over himself to cover his escape back up the canyon trail. If they had been listening instead of shouting, they might have heard his demented snickering.

Essy was back in a few moments. "Whoever it was, they're long gone now."

The moans from Griffin, who lay curled up on his side, brought their attention back to their wounded friend. Kneeling beside him, Raz grasped the arrow. Singed hairs identified the point of entry, but there was no blood. Raz tugged on the shaft, plucking the arrow out. "Strange," he noted quizzically. "There's no blood or wound. Just the charred hair and black spot."

Griffin shivered violently—eyes frozen, blankly staring straight ahead. Ryann looked on, wide-eyed from the startling event that had just occurred. The red fox continued to shake. Griffin was the senior individual in the group. Now everyone would be looking to Ryann for direction.

Raz persistently attended to Griffin, speaking encouraging words in his ear, listening to his chest, and inspecting the arrow's point of entry. After another few moments he spoke to the group. "That was no ordinary arrow. It's not affecting him physically, externally, or internally, as far as I can tell. But it is impacting his spirit. Somehow it has touched his soul and is causing him great pain."

"Wha…what can we do, Raz?" Terell asked, clearly shaken by the recent turn of events.

"I don't think there's anything we can do, but pray and wait it out. In the meantime, let's try and keep him as comfortable as possible."

"How 'bout we go back into one of these crevices and take turns as lookouts. We can watch two at a time," Ryann suggested. "Raz and I will go first. We'll need our rest for tomorrow. At first light we can figure out how to position ourselves for the best defense against Drake and his army."

Ryann thought it was unnerving the way Griffin shook, while at the same time his eyes were wide open, staring blankly in one direction. While Raz and he positioned their backs against the rocky face of the sheer canyon walls, Ryann wondered if he would be strong enough to stand before the dark army. This was their hour of need. He looked up toward the heavens and prayed for protection.

"Ryann, wake up!" Terell called out, shaking him at the same time.

"Huh? What? Oh, what time is it?" Ryann struggled to orient himself to his surroundings.

"I don't know. It's hard to tell with the way the grayness has set in, but it has to be early morning by how far we can see now."

Ryann glanced around. The walls on both sides of the reddish-tan canyon were visible. He looked west, in the direction from which they had come. The thin pathway snaked up into a darker haze. To the east, the canyon widened as far as he could see, which was only about one hundred feet.

"How's Griffin?"

"He came out of it about an hour ago," Terell answered, "while I was on watch. He was pretty shaken up, but he thinks he's ready to go again."

"That's good to hear. Let's get everyone together. We need to move away from here, down the canyon, to see if there's another way out."

Griffin appeared to be normal again on the outside, except for the small black spot where the arrow hit. Despite his reassurances to everyone that he was okay, his eyes jumped about nervously, and Ryann wondered if he'd be much help to the group during their next encounter. He wished there was time to rest and take it easy, but with Lord Ekron, Drake, and their army encamped up in the sand dunes they had to get moving. Alert to the edge of the jagged walls several hundred feet above them and any enemy that may be lurking, the weary travellers began negotiating the canyon floor to the east.

Ryann led the way, his staff held out front, stepping precariously on the loose gravel scattered across the smooth, gray, rock floor of the canyon. His mind wandered to thoughts of an old dried-up river, then snapped back to the ordeal at hand. He knew they were outnumbered, at least a thousand to one, and more than likely their only chance was to find an exit out of the back of the gorge.

Rays from the desert sun tried to break through the dark veil that had been cast over the region. With limited sunlight, the remaining beams cast eerie shadows down the steep cliffs. Heavy breathing and the occasional rock that was kicked aside from a weary foot were the only sounds that broke the silence. Terell moved up to the front, next to Ryann.

"D...do you think we'll find a way out?" he asked.

"I'm sure we will, Terell, I don't believe the Word would direct us this far for nothing."

"Uh, uhh, Ryann?"

"Yeah."

"Is that more haze up ahead or another wall?"

Ryann squinted for a better look into the misty air in front of them. A few more steps and Terell's question was answered. A dead end blocked any hopes of an exit. They stopped; one at a time, as they realized the gravity of their situation. Out of the uncomfortable silence, a voice bellowed from the skies.

"You might as well stop trying to get away, Ryann. We have you completely surrounded!"

Tingles crept up Ryann's spine as Drake's taunting bounced off the walls from every direction. He wondered if everyone else felt the same way.

Each of them looked up. Directly ahead and as far as they could see, black cloaked figures lined the ridges along both sides of the canyon walls. There was no way out. They were trapped.

"W...wha...what are we gonna do?" Terell mumbled.

Ryann had an idea. It was the thing that had been gnawing at him since Liddy had mentioned her horn.

"Everyone circle around Liddy facing outward," Ryann directed.

Quickly moving into place, they kept careful watch for any arrows from above. "Liddy, I want you to blow the horn seven times with a few seconds between each blast."

"What? Ryann. You're not thinking—"

"Liddy, we don't have time to think. Do it *now!*"

Liddy drew in a deep breath while bringing the horn up to her mouth. Her puffy cheeks blew as hard as they could into the ancient horn.

Ryann watched all the members in his group as they shifted uneasily. He wondered what effect it was going to have on Drake's army. Looking above, he noticed the stiff, dark figures begin to move and mill about.

"Hold your places!" Drake ordered. "You aren't afraid of a little horn are you?" His voice jumped around the canyon walls as most of the cloaked figures stopped moving.

Baaaaawwwaaaaa!

"Please, Ryann. Spare us the insult. Is that the best you have?" Drake challenged.

Baaaaawwwaaaaa!

Liddy's cheeks were tingling now as she took in another big gulp of air and blew again.

Baaaaawwwaaaa!

"My army is already pouring into the canyon at the west end," Drake announced. "It's just a matter of time before you surrender."

Baaaaawwwaaaaa!

"Come on…come on…just a few more times," Terell overheard Ryann muttering.

Baaaaawwwaaaaa!

Liddy's face was flushed pink from her long-winded blows, and her cheeks burned brightly.

"One last time, Liddy, then everyone scream as loud as you can," Ryann directed.

"You're doomed, Ryann Watters. Do—"

Baaaaawwwaaaa!

Liddy's horn drowned out the end of Drake's question. As she finished, the six screamed in unison with all the energy they could bring forth into this final stand. "Aaaaahhhhhhhhhhhhhhh!" Drake broke the silence. "What? What, is that it?" He mocked his schoolmate. "Let's hear some more, Liddy. Ha ha haaaa!"

The first rumble was barely audible. Then came the unmistakable reverberation of the earth shaking under their feet as the rumbles grew louder.

Whump!

A section of the cliff began to fall.

Whump! Whump!

Then two more! Suddenly the entire cliff at the dead end stripped off the face and thundered down. Screams from the army above filled the air as dark figures turned and ran to escape the avalanche. The earth quaked again and more rock fell from the walls on either side and behind them. Dust roiled skyward.

Drake gave the order to retreat only moments after the dispersing had begun.

Ryann watched in stunned silence as the army fled like a receding tide. The great victory was that they had planted fear in their hearts. Falling to their knees, they huddled together for protection and to keep out the blinding dust that was falling to the ground. Blinking rapidly to clear their eyes, they viewed the changed landscape. Raz was the first to speak.

"Look, up ahead. A hole in the cliff."

Raz scrambled anxiously across the rocky path and up the newly created rubble to an opening halfway up the cliff. He hesitated briefly then peered into the small four-foot opening.

"It looks like a cavern," he yelled down. "Come on up!"

Still nervous about a potential enemy that might have stayed around, they clambered with a sense of urgency over the rocks up to Raz. Gathering at the dark hole, Liddy stuck her head in. "How are we going to see anything?"

"I...I've got the pocket flashlight you gave me, Liddy!" Terell announced.

Terell fumbled in his pocket for the flashlight. While doing so, he noticed Ryann's ring. "Hey, Ryann! Ya...your ring...i...it's orange!"

Ryann brought his hand up for everyone to see. "Has it ever been that color before, Ryann?" Raz asked.

"Never."

"Maybe it's because we're close to the sword!" Liddy said giddily.

Terell turned on his flashlight and poked it into the opening. "It's a cavern all right. Who's first?"

"I'll go first," Ryann said. "Then everyone else follow me. Essy, you and Griffin stay behind and guard the opening. It's small enough that you could probably hold off an entire army. They'd have to come in one at a time."

Ryann bent down and pulled himself through the hole. Terell stayed at the entrance, pointing his flashlight in, as one by one they made their way into the dimly lit cavern.

CHAPTER 18

Sword-Seeker

YANN'S RING CAST an eerie orange glow that wasn't able to penetrate the full blackness of the cave. It did, however, provide enough illumination that they could see one another and about ten feet around them. Terell's small flashlight was just the opposite, piercing the darkness with a narrow beam of light to the nearby walls, yet not broad enough to open up their full surroundings.

"Terell, lead the way with your light. It can at least reveal anything out in front of us. My ring will provide us with enough light to see each other," Ryann said while stepping aside so Terell could move in front. Liddy and Raz moved in close behind and the group of four cautiously ambled off in the same easterly direction. Terell shifted his beam of light back and forth across the hard ground in front of them, touching the walls on both sides. With each footstep the solid rock beneath them built up their confidence. Ryann had expected it to not only be dark, but also damp in the cave. Instead, the air was musty like an old clothes closet that hadn't been opened in years and as dry as the desert they had left behind. With each passing moment they found themselves further away from the safety of the entrance and the outside world.

Ryann called out over his shoulder, "Essy? Griffin? Is everything still okay back there?" Echoes bounced off the tunnel walls, garbling his question. Then silence.

"Are we that far away? Maybe Drake regrouped and they've been captured!" Ryann thought.

Ryann kept his shifting thoughts to himself, not wanting to alarm the others. The shuffling of their feet in short, choppy steps to stay steady and their heavy breathing made up the only sounds as they forged ahead. The blackness fought against the one beam of light and Ryann's ring to beat down the small amount of hope they had.

"Whoa!" Terell cried out, causing them to stop abruptly, bunching into one another. "La...la...look!"

He flashed the light in an arc around his head, revealing the rugged dark stone walls and ceiling of the tunnel. Bringing the light down in front of him, he gasped as the end of the tunnel opened up into an ocean of blackness. "E...eh...everyone grab hands. We need to move ah...ahead slowly," Terell announced, pointing his flashlight at the ground just in front of them. His light no longer reached the cave walls. Instead, it traveled out into the blackness and then ended like driving off a cliff in the middle of the night. The limited security the walls of the tunnel had provided was gone. Each of them clenched their hands involuntarily to feel the person next to them.

"Ouch!" Liddy cried out as Raz's claws dug into the palm of her hand.

Raz quickly loosened his grip. "My apologies!"

"Let's go," Ryann said, leading the group out into empty black space. And then Ryann heard it.

"Turn back...death...darkness..."

It was a voice that would chill you to the bones, a voice that was icy-cold.

Ryann stumbled, but held tightly to Terell. The others were tugged by Terell.

"Ryann, what are you doing?"

"That voice. Can't you hear it?" Ryann asked.

"Turn back...death...evil..."

"Listen!" said Ryann urgently. Terell, Liddy, and Raz froze, still holding hands. A cold chill made its way down Ryann's spine, in the form of a tingling finger.

"Death...evil...destruction..."

"Can't you hear it?" Ryann asked again, swatting around himself with the staff in his one free hand.

"Hear what?" Liddy questioned.

The voice grew fainter.

"There was a voice. It said, 'Turn back, death, evil, and destruction.'"

"I heard nothing, and my ears are very acute," Raz offered.

Ryann recalled a verse he had read in Psalms: "Even though I walk through the valley of the shadow of death, I will fear no evil, for you are with me; your rod and your staff, they comfort me."

"That's it!" Ryann shouted.

"Wh...wha...what's it?" Terell asked.

"My staff," Ryann voiced excitedly. "I've been so preoccupied with getting into the cave and the darkness that I forgot about the very thing Gabriel gave me to help in searching for the sword—my staff!"

"Brilliant," Raz said.

Ryann let go of Terell's hand and gently pushed down halfway on button two.

Psshhhh!

A small flame flashed out of the end of his staff, illuminating the area in front of them and beyond.

Raz took his time to peer in every direction. "It is well known that animals have better eyesight than humans. Let me see if there is anything out of the ordinary we should be aware of."

"Well?" Liddy asked, a few moments later.

"There is a small, mmmm—"

"What?" Liddy asked.

"It appears as if there is small opening in the cavern wall…way off to the east," Raz answered.

"Then let's head that way," Ryann motioned. "Raz, you come up alongside me and let us know if it gets any clearer to you."

Travel by firelight was much easier. Without fear of surprises in the darkness or stumbling on the rocky cave floor, they were able to move at a brisk walk. Each of them opened their eyes as wide open as possible, straining to see what Raz had mentioned.

"Can you see it now?" Raz asked. "There's a door-like opening in the wall just ahead."

"I think I can just make out a white haze in front of us," Ryann answered. Each step brought the misty aura into focus.

"I can see it now!" Liddy cried out. "It looks like…like another tunnel. But what's lighting it up?"

Another fifty feet and it was clear to all of them. The tunnel piercing the cave wall was emitting a glowing white that beckoned them into it, like bugs to a porch light. Ryann couldn't decide if the light was really that bright or if the darkness from the cavern made it appear brighter than it was.

"Maybe it's a trap," Liddy said.

Ryann checked his ring. The orange glow was brighter than before. "I don't think so. My ring is glowing brighter. It may be another test—like the noises I heard before—to scare us away from the sword."

Ryann released the button on his staff. His flame flickered, then extinguished itself in a puff of smoke. The soft white glow from the entrance to the cave bathed the roughly carved walls in enough light for them all to see. His pulse quickened. Ryann sensed the sword was close—he could feel its grip in his hand and envisioned himself marching out of the cave in victory. Locked in place, he basked in the gentle light, drifting into a trance.

"Ryann?" Raz whispered.

"Huh? What? Yes," he finally managed, snapping out of his hypnotic state.

"The Word says to 'guard your heart for it is the wellspring of life.' You have been putting His words into your heart for the past few months. Listen to your heart and trust those words as we enter. It may very well be the difference between success and failure."

"Sure, Raz," Ryann muttered, stepping into the tunnel, which bathed him fully in the light. Terell hesitated, watching to see if something might happen to Ryann, and then turned toward Liddy and Raz, shrugged, and stepped in after him. Liddy, then Raz, quickly followed. Each of them realized separately as they moved through the tunnel that the light was coming from a much larger opening fifteen to twenty feet in front of them. Charging ahead purposefully, but cautiously, they gathered at the second opening and peered out. Terell glanced over his shoulder to make sure no one was following them.

The cavern was so massive that at first Ryann thought they had exited the cave altogether and that they were back out in the midnight sky. There were no stars in this sky, only a single beam of light flowing down out of the darkness.

"Look!" Ryann cried out, pointing slightly downward where the light ended. "The sword!"

All eyes focused on the brightly lit sword, golden handle up and the gleaming silver blade pointing to the ground. Primarily focused on the beauty of the sword itself, it was moments before they realized it was suspended in mid-air. Raz said what they all were thinking, "There doesn't appear to be anything holding the sword up."

"Unless the light itself is holding it up," Ryann answered. Streaming out of an endless black sky, the beacon of golden light flowed straight down to the sword, ending at the ground just beneath it. Sparkles of snappy light, like fireflies in a dusky Midwest sky, popped on and off around the sword.

"Theoretically, that's impossible," Liddy responded.

"Mmmm, that's probably why it's happening," Ryann answered, a small grin forming.

"What?" Liddy questioned.

Ryann let her ponder his response. After all they had been through, he didn't expect the sword to just be laying there, waiting for him to stroll over and pick it up. No, getting here was a challenge, and he was sure it wasn't over yet.

As the fascination with the suspended sword faded, their eyes were drawn to the surrounding area. Soft, white light emanating from the glowing sword provided enough light to view the cave floor between the sword and where they stood. Behind the sword and on both sides the ground was pitch black. Ryann was reminded of his favorite fishing hole on Lake Franklin and the thin peninsula of land protruding out into the lake where they fished. Florida sunshine forced the dirty brown waters of Lake Franklin to sparkle on the surface. Here in the cave the pale glowing light revealed only degrees of darkness.

"Wow!" Ryann mouthed.

"W...wha...what now?" Terell asked.

"Let's move down to the walkway that goes out to the sword," Ryann suggested. "Be ready for anything."

Sloping gently down, the rocky cavern met a strip of land forming a bridge out to the island over which the sword was hanging. Stepping cautiously down the hill, they remained tense, ready for any challenges they might face. Gathering at the foot of the hill, the three humans and one raccoon gathered in a circle to assess the situation.

An inky sea surrounded a narrow pathway jetting out toward the island. Halfway into the black lake, the path split to the left and right, with both trails leading to opposite sides of the illuminated island. Four sets of eyes went every direction, but there didn't appear to be any other way out onto the island, except by way of the paths. On the island, a smooth, pyramid-shaped hill led up to a tiny precipice from which the sword hovered.

"The trails are only wide enough for us to go out in single file," Ryann observed. "I'll go first; then Terell, you follow me; then Liddy; then Raz, you come last."

Ryann took two steps out onto the path, then hesitated, turning to make sure they were all following. As Terell's foot came down on the path, the ground began to shake and a low rumble echoed into the chamber. "Back! Back!" Ryann shouted. Terell and he jumped back off the path to Liddy and Raz. The ground was still again.

"That's odd," Raz said. "Ryann, walk back out on the path again."

Ryann cautiously stepped out to where he had stopped previously. Nothing. The ground stayed firmly in place, and the air was silent.

"Okay. Now walk back. Terell, you step out and take his place."

Ryann moved back to the mainland area and Terell stepped out. As his foot pressed into the soil, the ground under his feet began shaking, and the rumbling bellowed out of the darkness. When Terell jumped back, it stopped.

"Interesting. Now, Liddy, you try to step out on the pathway," Raz instructed.

Liddy smiled when she took her first step and nothing happened. As she lifted her other foot to take a second step the ground began to tremble, and she quickly rejoined the group. Raz scampered out onto the pathway with the same result. Coming back to Ryann, he gave his assessment. "It appears, Ryann, that the task you have been given, to retrieve the King's sword, is for you and you alone."

"Is there anything else we can deduce from this, Raz?"

"I cannot say for certain, but I believe all of the circumstances that have led you here have been based more on what is inside of you rather than what is on the outside."

"Like what I'm thinking?"

Raz rubbed his hairy chin with his curved black claws. "No. I think it's deeper than that. As I mentioned before, what is in your heart matters most. I am convinced that your success in attaining the sword will be linked to the deepest beliefs in your heart."

Ryann glanced down at his ring while Raz spoke. It was glowing white. When Raz finished, Ryann considered his words. He knew they were true and that he was going to have to think carefully about what his course of action would be. Gazing into the eyes of his raccoon friend, his first friend in Aeliana, Ryann said, "Thanks, Raz."

"Terell, here. You take my staff. I think it has served its purpose of getting me to this point."

Ryann returned to face the path, the black sea, and the hill beyond, crowned with the prize. Lowering himself to one knee, he bowed his head and closed his eyes. His parents had taught him to cleanse his heart before partaking in the sacraments at church. Breathing in deeply, he recounted his actions of the past week, confessing from his heart everything he had done wrong. He recounted some of the verses he had read from Proverbs that week. Raz, Terell, and Liddy stood around Ryann, each of them with a hand on his shoulder for support. Moving in closer, they listened to Ryann's whispered prayer: "Wisdom will save you from the ways of wicked men, from men whose words are perverse, who leave the straight paths to walk in dark ways, who delight in doing wrong and rejoice in the perverseness of evil, whose paths are crooked…I must trust in the Lord with all my heart and lean not on my own understanding; in all my ways acknowledge him, and he will make my paths straight."

There was a pale white aura about his face as he stepped off the mainland down the path to the sword. Ryann shook his head to clear his mind, forcing himself to focus on the task at hand. Concentrating on attaining his goal, he pushed his friends into the far corners of his mind. Again he took several deep breaths and exhaled slowly. Each step was going to bring him closer to his objective. His first instinct was to run as fast as he could toward the sword, but his heart told him to be cautious and use wisdom.

Fifty paces down the narrow path, he came to the split in the trail. Ryann looked from one to the other, considering his options. The first path went off to the left and bent around until it came to one side of the island. The other went off to the right and curved haphazardly around until it came to the other side of the island. There were no noteworthy differences between the two.

Dropping down to one knee on the rocky path, Ryann peered into the blackness off to the left of him. "It's so dark," he thought. "What could it be?" Picking up a small pebble, he tossed it into the darkness. It disappeared into the black without a ripple. Ryann listened intently. Silence. Reaching out, he slowly stuck his hand into the blackness. His hand disappeared, completely absorbed. It's not water! It feels like nothing, like air, but it's gone. Tingles began running through his fingers like little ant bites. Before he could pull back, a chill crept along his fingertips up to his wrist. "Yah!" Ryann yelped, pulling his hand away like he had touched a hot stove.

There didn't appear to be a bottom to it, only empty space. Which way? The groans he heard were coming from him.

"Think! Raz had said guard my heart because it was the well-spring of life, and I had put his Word into it," he thought. Later on he had found Raz's words of wisdom in Proverbs, chapter four to be exact. Following that verse there was more advice about guarding your heart.

"Let your eyes look straight ahead, fix your gaze directly before you. Make level paths for your feet and take only ways that are firm. Do not swerve to the right or the left; keep your foot from evil."

"So if I shouldn't take the right or the left path, which way do I go? Straight?" Ryann thought. He had stuck his hand in the blackness to the left. Ryann stared intently into the sea of blackness pooled straight ahead between him and the island. It looked the same and probably felt the same. He still held his tingling hand. "Maybe I can try an experiment like Raz," he thought. Picking up three more pebbles, he tossed one onto the path heading off to the left. He expected it to bounce, but was surprised to watch it vanish. Turning to the other path he tossed another pebble, again assuming it to bounce off the hard trail. The pebble passed straight through the ground. Strange! Gazing into the dark ground in front of him, as if the path continued...Ryann dropped the last pebble.

Dink...Dink.

It bounced twice and settled on top of the blackness as if it was floating in space. Reaching down, he touched the black ground around the pebble. Instead of his hand disappearing, it felt like the same rocky texture of the path he had been walking on. He continued pressing down on the hidden trail, to the left and right, until his hand found the edges. It's an illusion! The hidden path heading straight ahead was the same as the one he had been travelling on, yet it was covered in the same blackness that made up the black lake. Grabbing a handful of pebbles, Ryann tossed them out onto the darkness in front of him. The little rocks scattered about, settling on top of the mirage, revealing the hidden path.

Far behind him, Terell, Liddy, and Raz watched in horror as Ryann stepped straight off the path.

Liddy screamed. "Ryann. Nooooo!"

Focusing on the small rocks highlighting his pathway over the black emptiness, Ryann blocked out everything around him. Cautiously moving to the point where the pebbles ended, he reached in to his pocket and grabbed another fistful of rocks. Again he tossed them out in front of himself to reveal the next section of path. After the fourth scattering, Ryann reached a point that he could hop onto the island.

"He didn't hear you, yet he continues to walk across the blackness," Raz noted as they watched what appeared to be Ryann walking on black water. "He sees what we do not see. Very good. Ryann is listening to his heart."

The sword gleamed magnificently. Illumination from the sparkling beam of light shining down from heaven pierced through the darkness and highlighted the treasure awaiting him on top of the pyramid. Screams filled the distant air behind him, tearing at Ryann's focus as he marveled at the vision in front of him. Desperately tempted to turn around and look back, he wondered if the Word was tempting him. Paralyzed as he dwelled on this thought, he startled at a voice speaking clearly in his head, "When tempted, no one should say, the Word is tempting me. For the Word cannot be tempted by evil, nor does he tempt anyone; but each one is tempted when, by his own evil desire, he is dragged away and enticed." Ryann's resolve tightened. Resisting the temptation to turn around and find out where the screams were coming from, he looked up at the glittering sword. As quickly as they came, the screams died away, replaced by the echoes of cascading rocks. Was an avalanche caving in on his friends? "I can't look back. I need to focus on the sword," he reminded himself. He closed his eyes briefly, summoning a verse that he had stored up in his heart, "Forgetting what is behind and straining toward what is ahead,

I press on toward the goal to win the prize for which God has called me."

From a distance, the pyramid the sword was hovering above did not appear to be an obstacle. Up close, it was obvious to Ryann that it was going to be challenging to get to the top. At least twenty feet high, smooth, and at a steep angle. Ryann knew there was no way to climb up this edifice to get the sword. He listened intently for anything suspicious as he moved around the three-sided pyramid. His examinations weren't bringing about immediate results, but he knew there must be a way to the top and more than likely it was going to be more of a mental than physical challenge.

Ryann admired the sword glistening in the sparkling light. As he moved around the pyramid, the hilt and blade rotated with his movement. The first two sides were identical flat, smooth sandstone with no indentations. Upon reaching the third side, he immediately noticed that while there was a similar texture on the face, there was one obvious difference. Standing horizontally, about waist high for Ryann, were seven inlaid metal squares. Each brass square was approximately six inches by six inches in dimension and numbered one through seven. Above the numbers was a plaque, of the same metal, with letters partially covered with sand. Ryann moved closer and blew several times to clear the grit. He slowly read the words:

> Two are better than one.
> If one falls down, two can help him up.
> A cord of three strands is not quickly broken.
> There are four things that never say, "Enough!"
> Five smooth stones.
> Six things the Word hates,
> Seven that are detestable to Him.
> Which number completes your quest?
> Choose wisely...you may only choose one time!

It made no sense to him. "I have to choose one of the seven numbers from that?" Ryann tried to understand the meaning of the words as he read them aloud again. "Two is better than one…that has to eliminate one, doesn't it? Three strands are not quickly broken…okay, that's a good thing. Four things never say enough. That sounds stubborn to me. Five smooth stones? How many stones did David pick up to fight Goliath? The Word hates six things and seven are detestable…they both sound bad." Ryann ran through them again. "Okay, it looks like one, four, six, and seven are definitely out. That leaves two, three, and five. Mmm, it sounds like two is good, but three is better. What's special about five smooth stones?" Ryann tried to recall everything that had happened to him in Aeliana, something that might include numbers or counting.

He considered his circle of friends. There were three of them if he included himself. And it did say that three are not quickly broken. He smacked himself on the head. Who could forget the three blue moons that came together as one when he first heard the Word speak? He looked at the pyramid again. Was it a coincidence that there were three sides? Ryann mulled all of his conclusions over again. "I wonder," he mumbled, while raising the ring up and placing it in front of the number three. It changed from orange to bright white—truth! He slowly moved it to the right so it was over the number four. His ring began changing again. At first it changed back to orange. It flickered white then changed again—blood red. Danger!

Ryann moved his ring across the other numbers; all of them remained red. Three! It had to be three! Ryann reached out with his ring hand, surprised to see the visible shaking, and set his hand on the number three. His ring turned white and he pushed the metal square.

Grrrrr…Shzzzz…Clunk!

The grinding of gears turning, metal shifting, and weights banging caused Ryann to step back cautiously, his eyes scanning up and down the pyramid. He moved around the pyramid to where the noises were coming from. Perfectly formed bronze stairs were now inset into one of the smooth sides from the bottom to the top. Ryann tested the first step. It was firm under his foot. One foot after another he made his way tentatively up the side until the sword came into view. There was enough room at the top of the pyramid for him to stand alongside his prize.

The sword glimmered more beautifully up close. Ryann gazed up the sparkling, translucent beam shining down from above. He still couldn't tell where it was coming from. With a purposeful, yet humble motion, Ryann moved his hand slowly into the light. It was just the opposite of the blackness. His skin glowed and a warmth began spreading down his fingers, into his arm, and then across his body. Power swelled within him and he felt like he could leap off the pyramid in one mighty jump. Ryann watched his own hand, mesmerized as the popping sparkles danced around and on his skin. His fingers closed on the grip and he pulled.

CHAPTER 19

Gabriel's
Return

ABLUR OF ENERGY rushed through Ryann's body, causing him to tense up as he pulled the weapon free from its invisible scabbard. Squeezing the grip firmly, he slashed all around him like he was fighting an imaginary beast. Ryann had expected the sword to feel heavy in his hand, not light and airy, as if it were meant for him. Caught up in the revelry of achieving his goal, Ryann almost forgot about his friends. Turning to look across the cavern, he spotted them and held the sword up high as a sign of victory.

Retracing their trail back to the main cave went by quickly with Terell leading the way. Holding the staff up high, like a torch, its flame cast a glow broadly around them, pushing away the darkness. Having the sword in Ryann's hand calmed everyone's spirit, knowing they had accomplished the lofty goal of finding the sword. Ryann replayed the excited, cheering faces of Terell, Liddy, and Raz over and over again in his mind. His steps were lighter than before. He felt as if the energy and passion that had been imparted to him when he first touched the sword were still inside.

Approaching the cave entrance, Liddy called out, "Essy! Griffin!"

"Aye, we're here!" they heard Griffin's familiar voice call back.

Reunited, they hugged one another before Essy and Griffin begged to hear the details. "I can tell you all about it while we travel back," Ryann stated, fully energized and ready to race back to Myraddin.

"It's almost night," Terell noted, weary from their endeavor. "Why don't you tell the story now while we rest within the protection of the cave, and then we can head out under the cover of darkness."

"Great idea, Terell. Maybe I'm a little too anxious after all the excitement!" Ryann grinned at Terell.

"I concur," Griffin added, settling in with the group to hear the trials of getting to the sword.

Two glaring eyes watched the six figures drop down from the hole in the cliff to the canyon floor. Hidden in the darkness, the remains of Drake's army lined the length of one side of the canyon. Half of the army had been lost in the rubble from the avalanche or run off in fear, an action for which they would have to answer to Lord Ekron. Drake knew he would have to do the same if he failed to stop Ryann. Heading off to stir up other uprisings elsewhere in Aeliana, the dark angel had left him to wait for Ryann and his friends to exit the cave. Once again Drake would have the element of surprise; however, this time he needed to take advantage of it. Holding his stomach, he thought he was going to be sick as it churned with a wicked concoction of anticipation and angst. Turning away from his men, Drake hunched over a boulder and vomited.

"*Whooo. Whooo,*" Drake called out using the designated owl signal he had given his men to light their arrows. He waited a few moments, viewing the tense arm muscles in those closest to him, bowstrings tightly drawn. Then he gave the third "hoot" for them to release. Thirty-nine flaming arrows streaked across the sky, raining down upon the unsuspecting travelers.

Ryann and Terell led the way, with Essy and Liddy following in the center, and Griffin and Raz bringing up the rear. Ryann held the weightless sword firmly in his grip. Terell held the staff up high, pressing down halfway on button two. The flickering flame cast a glow around them, which pressed back against the black-drenched canyon. They walked in silence under the moonless night, except for the lone hoot of an owl.

"That's odd," Ryann broke the silence. "I didn't realize owls hoot in Aeliana. I thought all animals could talk…"

Raz hesitated, listening more intently. On the next hoot he cried out his warning, "That's not an owl. Terell, turn out the flame and run."

Flaming arrows illuminated the sky as they arched high overhead, then began descending toward them. "Terell, point the staff up and push button three!" Ryann yelled amidst the confusion.

Bssshhhhhhh!

A torrent of cold blasted into the nighttime air, forming a shield of ice over their heads. Flaming arrows buried themselves into the surrounding sand while others became a whiff of smoke as they extinguished themselves in the wall of ice.

Drake's eyes flashed black and red as he watched the scene unfold. Covering himself in his cloak of darkness, he stormed down the pathway into the canyon.

"This strategy isn't going to last forever," Ryann said. "Raz, you, Griffin, and Essy, pray for the Word to deliver us from this evil."

Ryann moved closer to Liddy and whispered quietly. "I'm sure the ice shield won't last much longer."

"Do you see any way out of this?" she asked.

"Well, something's been nagging at me since we left the cave. What does *reprieve* mean?"

"Ryann, this is not time for games," Liddy answered, putting her hands on her hips.

"Liddy, I'm serious. This may be important!"

"*Reprieve* means 'to get help or assistance,'" she answered impatiently. "So what?"

"Mmm, inside the cave, the words on the plaque by the sword said, 'Three brings reprieve.'"

"Three what?" Liddy asked.

"Well, I'm guessing here, but the horn has helped us in lot of ways. One long blast created fear, and seven short blasts brought down the cliff walls," Ryann recounted. "I want you to give three short blasts on the horn. I think that might bring us help."

"You're right, that is a wild guess, Ryann," Liddy responded.

"You have a better one?"

Liddy put the horn up to her lips and blew one loud, but short blast.

Bwwwaaa!

Raz's, Essy's, and Griffin's eyes popped open from praying.

Bwwwaaa!

The horn rang out for the second time. Arrows plunked into the ground around them and glanced off the ice covering overhead.

"Do you think it's going to work?" Terell asked, having overheard their conversation.

"It's worth a shot."

Bwwwaaa!

Liddy's face flushed pink as she pulled the horn away from her pursed lips.

Rumble... Rumble...

"What was that?" Liddy asked, over the last-gasp sputtering of the staff.

"It sounds like, like thunder," Ryann answered.

Rumble... Rumble... Splash!

Grape-sized drops of rain pelted the rocky canyon floor, exploding into little fountain bursts as they leapt back up into the air. The staff gave one last gasp and extinguished itself, despite Terell's thumb frantically pressing any of the buttons. Freshly lit arrows screaming across the sky were smothered out and batted to the ground as the rain poured down from above. For a moment everyone's hair stood on end, then—

Crack!

Lightning flashed in a dazzling spectacle of jagged bolts zig-zagging from the heavens down to the earth. Ryann peered up at the illuminated sky for the three or four seconds it flashed.

Wings flapped several times from a glowing white figure. Was it? Could it be? Did the horn really call Gabriel to help us or maybe the prayers? Questions flowed through Ryann's brain like turbulent rapids down a rushing river. Ryann waited for the next flash.

"Look up in the sky! I think I saw Gabriel!" Ryann called out.

All eyes strained into the darkness, hoping it was true. Thunder cracked, and the sky lit up again in a radiant array of energy slashing its way haphazardly to the ground. In the midst of the golden backdrop, a powerful white angel hovered in the sky, his arm raised high, holding a gleaming sword. Ryann was the only one who had met Gabriel and recognized him at once. Out of respect, he thrust his sword skyward. The lightening crashing downward redirected itself toward Ryann, melding into his upheld sword. In a quick, brilliant flash, hundreds of bolts shot out of Ryann's sword toward the enemy on the cliffs.

Cries of anguish rang out as hooded figures were shocked, singed, and knocked off their feet. Shouts of victory sounded behind him as the enemy ran off and Ryann dropped his arm, still in shock from what had happened.

"Ryann, are you okay?" Liddy asked, reaching out tentatively to touch his arm.

Ryann smiled weakly to answer her.

"That was awesome, buddy," Terell said, slapping his friend on the back. Raz, Essy, and Griffin gathered around Ryann to offer their congratulations as the thunder drifted away and the raindrops slowed to a mild pitter-patter.

"I must applaud you as well, young Ryann," Griffin said. "I had my doubts when you first came before the council. However, you have proven yourself a noble warrior in this quest."

Ryann's ears burned, self-conscious of all the attention he was getting.

"You have listened to your heart, Ryann, and responded with great strength of character," Raz added.

Ryann was embarrassed by such glowing comments, but he had so much admiration for Raz, who was his first contact in Aeliana, that he savored the remark. Out of what had become a habit, Ryann glanced down at his ring. It was red—danger!

A familiar voice that still raised the hair on the back of his neck boomed from behind him. "Turn around slowly, Ryann, unless you want to experience what your fox friend did from one of my flaming arrows."

Drake was back.

Ryann rotated slowly, careful not to make any sudden movements. Drake was facing them twenty paces away, his bow fully drawn back with a fiery arrow locked in place. Ryann had his sword in hand, not that it would do him much good at this distance. His concern was for everyone else in his group. Ryann cautiously glanced around without moving his head. None of Drake's henchmen were to be seen.

"Don't try looking for a way out this time, Ryann. Drop your sword. And Terell and Liddy, you drop your staff and horn," Drake ordered confidently.

For the first time, Ryann stared back at Drake without fear, matching his determination. Dark circles outlined Drake's eyes, making him look weary and drained. He spoke with confidence, but Ryann sensed fear was pushing him. "Fear of failing Lord Ekron," Ryann thought. He needed to exploit that fear.

"Drake, you can't win. You've chosen the losing side to begin with," Ryann spoke firmly without losing eye contact.

"Shut up, Ryann!" Drake spit, losing some of his composure. "Put your sword down, now!"

"Drake, you have to know that good always triumphs over evil in the end. Lord Ekron was created perfectly by the Word, but was then cast out of the heavens when he rebelled," Ryann responded to Drake in a calm voice, trying to get him off balance. "The created can never defeat the Creator."

"That's enough!" Drake shouted. "Put your weapons down now or Liddy's spirit will feel the cold fire of one of my arrows."

Ryann felt powerless, but knew there was power in the sword, as evidenced by the lightening flashing through it and targeting the enemy. Now he needed to have the faith to believe that it could do even more; things he hadn't seen with his eyes but that he believed in his heart the Word could do. In an instant, Ryann twirled the sword straight down and with both hands drove the tip as hard as he could into the rocky canyon floor. Mouths opened in shock as the travelers witnessed the sword piercing the solid rock like Ryann was sheathing it in a scabbard. As the sword penetrated, the Earth erupted with a thunderous crack and began rolling toward Drake, building upon itself like a massive tidal wave. Shattered rock splintered in every direction as the ground churned over and over on itself.

Drake's jaw quivered as he involuntarily opened his mouth to scream, but no sound came out. Spinning away he ran, pumping his arms and legs as hard as he could. They watched as Drake dropped his bow and flaming arrow in his haste to get away from the building steamroller of rock.

"Don't let him get away!" Ryann yelled back to Essy and Griffin. "Get him!" Leopard and fox blurred past him an instant later, on the offensive to hunt the hunter. Reaching its full height at some twenty feet in the air, the churning wave of rocks turned over and slammed into the hard canyon floor with an ear-splitting crunch.

Drake continued sprinting as fast as he could, looking up to see the wave of rocks curling over his head. At the last second, he threw himself forward out of the grasp of the pummeling boulders. Powdery dust and fragments from the shattered rocks filled the air in a suffocating shower. Essy and Griffin raced to the edge of the dusty mist and stopped, peering in for a glimpse of the enemy. Before the dust could settle, Drake pulled his cloak of darkness over himself. Then getting to his feet, careful so as not to disturb the unstable rubble and give himself away, Drake slinked away from the two animals intent on sniffing him out.

"He's not here!" Essy yelled back to Ryann and the others. "He's either buried in the rubble or made it out of the canyon." Moments latter, after the dust had fully settled, Essy and Griffin made a search around the perimeter of the wreckage and then headed back to meet up with everyone.

"That was the most amazing thing I've ever seen," Terell proclaimed, eyes still wide in bewilderment.

Liddy quickly added, "I have to say, Ryann, I was trying to get your attention to dive for cover at the same time, but I had no idea you were going to do that."

With a shrug of his shoulders, Ryann admitted, "Guys, to be honest, I had no idea that was going to happen. I wanted to stop Drake with all my heart, but I never envisioned the earth erupting like it did."

"The Word blesses those with a pure heart, Ryann. He has said that with faith the size of a mustard seed you can move mountains. Surely we witnessed real faith here today," Raz said, patting his good friend on the back.

Griffin helped them all focus, "Let's get moving. It's time we got back to Myraddin."

Heading west toward the castle, an eerie voice echoed off the canyon walls, reminding them that it wasn't over.

"Ryann, you may think you've won, but I'll be back, and when you least expect it."

The black veil of darkness had been lifted from Aeliana. A few of the rebels had returned, humbly asking for forgiveness and seeking to be restored with the Word. Many more hardened their hearts and moved deeper into the forests to feast on the twisted lies from Lord Ekron. Splotches of scorched earth still dotted the land here and there, but for the most part Aeliana's beauty had returned. Terell was amazed as they entered Myraddin.

"It's like a whole new world," he exclaimed, his head whirling about like a bobble-head, as he breathed in the vibrant aromas, vivid colors, and jovial chattering of the town citizens moving purposefully about.

"I can understand how you must feel, Terell." Liddy sighed. "This is your first time seeing Aeliana like it really is. For me the darkness we experienced when we arrived a few days ago was disheartening."

Approaching the castle within the city, Ryann was strangely quiet, "Yeah, but, something isn't quite the same," he finally said.

"What do you mean?" Liddy asked.

"I've been pondering that question the entire way back. It's the..." he hesitated, getting their full attention, "taste."

"Taste?" Terell and Liddy shot back in unison.

"Not exactly taste, like you and I typically think of it. But I remember coming here the first few times and the smells and colors were so..." he struggled to find the right words, "so overwhelming that I felt as if I could actually stick out my tongue and taste everything around me."

"Really?" Terell looked at him quizzically, sticking his tongue out and lapping at the air.

Liddy jabbed Terell in the ribs with her elbow.

"Hey! What was that for?"

"For making fun of Ryann," Liddy answered, nodding her head.

"I wasn't making fun of Ryann; I was just trying it out."

"He's right," Raz finally spoke as they came to a stop in front of the same castle entrance where they had first joined one another. The tunnel passage that seemed so ominous a few days earlier was bright and lively, inviting their entrance.

They all looked at Raz as Terell spoke, "What do you mean, he's right?"

"Griffin, Essy, and I all grew up in Aeliana, and we have been conferring quietly during our trek back to Myraddin. We have come to the conclusion that while everything appears to be back to normal, there is something that is not quite right."

"And that would be…" Terell trailed off, motioning with his hand for a response.

Essy cut in, "Something has been taken away from Aeliana. For a time we thought everything was back to normal, but the full richness of the smells, colors, and sounds is not the same. We concluded that it has something to do with the evil that entered with Lord Ekron and Drake and the rebellious spirit of some of our people."

Griffin weighed in at last. "I fear that we will no longer be able to experience the fullness of Aeliana like the Word intended for us. Perhaps it is a question that the council can address for us."

The fox did not wait for a response, but turned and trotted through the entrance. Ryann's ring glowed white, and the somber realization of the truth drained some of the excitement from their victorious quest. Silently they followed Griffin, one by one, into the castle.

Reaching their final destination, Ryann glanced around the room where they had left the High Council only a few short days ago. Rhythmically keeping time by tapping his foot, he breathed in the fresh air and colors that had replaced the dank muskiness from the first meeting.

Ushered in by a jovial badger, they took their places in a self-imposed line directly in front of the seven ornately carved chairs. Griffin was determined to remain with them and give the full report of their activities. Ryann held the sword loosely at his side, now so comfortable in his grip that it felt like an extension of his arm.

The soft moan of an ancient door slowly opening echoed through the high-peaked meeting room, announcing the council's entrance. In a manner reminiscent of their first encounter, the members strode confidently across the platform in an orderly line. Ryann looked from face to face as they took their positions; each wrinkled concern from the previous introduction was transformed into gentle, knowing smiles.

Aodan cleared his throat, addressing them with a raspy eloquence that reminded Ryann of a kindly grandfather. "I understand congratulations are in order." His eyes shifted ever so briefly to Ryann's sword before continuing. "However, there are a few things you must be made aware of. An ancient evil entered our land, which we have estimated, through encounters by our people, to be around the time Miss Lydia first came to Aeliana."

Ryann looked over at Liddy, the color draining from her face and her mouth opening to respond. Aodan raised his hand to cut her off, then continued, "We do not believe this to be an action for which you bear responsibility; however, the consequences are what we are left to deal with." Aodan allowed silence to fill the room.

Motioning toward the burly black bear seated to his right, Aodan backed into his center chair and settled into it. Standing to address everyone, the bear's hulking frame rose to a height of more than six feet. Grimacing slightly at his intimidating posture, Ryann thought he was someone you would not want to unexpectantly encounter in the woods at night.

"I have been travelling into the forest land to gather as many eyewitness accounts of what has been happening as I can," the bear announced. "Lord Ekron has convinced many of our people to join his side with promises to give them the desires of their heart. I encountered a hill dwarf and red dragon who had received gifts, yet neither appeared happy from my distant observation." When finished, he squeezed back down into his chair as Aodan rose to continue.

"Thank you, Worley. From now on, what one sees in Aeliana might not be what it appears to be on the outside. Innocence and purity have given way to wisdom and discernment. We will need to train our people in the way of the Word and how to use His power to defend themselves against Lord Ekron and his new followers. Even now, Aurelia, princess of the elfin clan, is assembling the annual messages of the Word into a book, which we will be able to distribute to the followers of the truth."

In an instant, Aodan's demeanor changed with the warmth of a smile spreading widely across his judicious face. "And now, let us celebrate the victory of the quest for the King's sword."

Aodan clapped his hands together, the lone sound ringing through the room. He followed it by another and another until the rest of the council joined in with applause for the successful adventurers.

Ryann felt himself blushing with the attention, but questions bounced around in his head, distracting him from the embarrassment. As the clapping subsided, Ryann spoke up, "Chancellor Aodan? Who is the King that I am returning the sword to? Will we meet Him?"

Aodan's bemused look changed abruptly to one deep in thought, as he reached up to run his wrinkled hands through his flowing white beard. "You will not return the sword to a King who will receive it now. The sword is for the future King whom the Word has foretold will come."

CHAPTER 20

Journey Home

ITTING ALONE IN the small chapel that formed the spiritual heart of Myraddin, Ryann dwelled on Aodan's last statement. Three sides of the room were covered in vibrantly stained glass. Sun rays streaming in cast a rainbow of color across the room. The sword had been taken to the castle armory and locked up. In some ways, Ryann was disappointed. He knew the sword wasn't his to keep, yet in a prideful way he now realized he had hoped to deliver it to a *real* king. Dwelling further on that thought, he stared at the myriad of colors that began dancing in front of him. Swirling slowly, then melding together into a ball of light, bright blues, reds, yellows, and greens faded to white. Ryann held up his hand to block the intense whiteness, until it began dimming to form a shape. He had experienced this before, his old fears now amazement as the being materialized before him. "Gabriel!" Ryann's voice echoed excitedly through the chapel.

"Well done, Ryann, thou hast completed the task set before you." Ryann smiled deeply, still taking in the purely clad whiteness in the form of this powerful angel in front of him. Gabriel's wings were folded behind him, his sweeping blond hair outlining a fearless yet caring face with piercing blue eyes gazing back. "But I thought I was finding the sword to give to a king now," Ryann replied.

"His ways are not our ways. His thoughts are not our thoughts," Gabriel responded rather stoically.

Ryann was not satisfied, "So, you don't have an answer for me?"

"I am a warrior and a messenger. I do not provide answers. That is for Him to provide in His way and timing."

"Well, at least let me thank you for helping me fight Drake in the midst of the electrical storm."

"You called out and He chose to answer by sending me. Your thanks should be to Him," Gabriel responded.

Ryann studied Gabriel's strong face and wondered if he was capable of feeling. His sparkling blue eyes seemed to indicate it was possible.

"The King is pleased with your service and will come soon, as He defines *soon*. Before that time comes, you are to seek out the shield of faith."

"Shield of faith? Where? Here in Aeliana?" Ryann rattled off.

"It is not for me to reveal," answered Gabriel calmly. "You shall find out in due time."

From his previous experiences with Gabriel, Ryann knew better than to ask for more clarification. Instead he inquired about Gabriel's assistance. "Will I get to keep the gifts you gave me?"

"Yes, thou may," Gabriel replied. "And with increased training comes an increase in wisdom. With increased wisdom comes an increase in power."

"I'll try to remember that. Do I just wait for the signal from the ring?"

"The Spirit will lead you, and the ring *may* open the way," the angel replied as he began floating backwards, the light peeling away with him.

Ryann blinked his eyes several times to clear the sparkling remnants. Staff firmly in hand, his horn around his side, Ryann looked down at his ring. It was glowing gold. "Time to go," Ryann thought, as he headed out to find Terell and Liddy.

Parting ways had not been easy in the past for Ryann and Liddy. Ryann shifted awkwardly back and forth from one foot to the other. "Well, I guess this is goodbye, for now," he quickly added. Extending his arm, he grasped the returning paw of Raz and shook.

"Ryann, I must say, it has been quite the adventure. I never could have imagined our exploits following our initial encounter that one bright morning. The Word has certainly increased my faith through the experience."

Fortunately for Terell, he was part of the longest, most difficult, and rewarding time in Aeliana. Unfortunately for him, he had built a strong bond with many of the citizens, especially Griffin. Terell stuck his hand out to Griffin, who returned the gesture. "Thanks for everything. I hope we get a chance to come back again."

"From what Ryann has said about his meeting with Gabriel, it would seem assured; however, from experience I know that the Word works things out in His perfect way, which is not always what we expect," Griffin responded.

Liddy's face glowed brightly with emotion as she viewed the exchanges taking place. Rushing forward, she opened her arms fully to hug the lean, muscular leopard. "Oh, Essy. I don't want to leave. This has been the most exciting time of my life!"

Essy purred, then added, "I agree, Liddy, our bond is strong. If we don't have the opportunity to meet again, we will have many good stories to tell."

Ryann almost didn't recognize the bubbling noise; it had become such a natural background sound to him. He peered down into the moat to confirm the beginnings of the glowing gold circle. Taking one last look at the majestic fortress and each of their animal friends, Ryann burned a mental image in his mind before delivering the inevitable news.

"It's time," he simply stated, nodding toward the water circling the castle.

On the far side of the western forests, deep in the recesses of the thick shadowy trees, Drake knelt on the rotting leaves. With clearing blue skies and the freshness of Aeliana slowly returning to a glimpse of its former self, Drake trudged deeper and deeper into shadows. Hiding in the darkness calmed his nerves. With no one around, he could be alone in his thoughts. He could do what he wanted without it being exposed for everyone to see. Or so he believed.

"You have failed me again!" Lord Ekron bellowed.

"Forgive me," Drake meekly responded without looking up.

"Ha! Forgive? I never forgive anyone. You should be thankful I am choosing to allow you to live!"

Drake dared to quickly peek up. Lord Ekron's eyes burned back into his, sending a chilly stream through his mind down into his chest. He shivered, then slumped further down into the putrid leaves, desperately trying to hold back the urge to weep bitterly.

"You are weak and of no use to me anymore. I am sending you back through the dark portal."

"Th…thank…you," Drake meekly responded in a raspy voice.

"Do not thank me. When you return to your land, you will not remember your time in Aeliana. But you will see me again. That is when you will pay for your failures."

Two days following their return to Mount Dora, Ryann and Terell were getting ready for another goodbye. Peddling their bicycles in the early morning sun, the boys raced past Heron Cay Lakeview Bed and Breakfast and skirted around Lake Dora on Lakeshore Drive. Whether Ryann was daydreaming or the humidity was affecting his effort, Terell didn't care; he was in the lead for a change. Approaching Oakland Lane, Ryann snapped out of daze, saw Terell ahead of him, and began peddling furiously. Terell glanced quickly over his shoulder as he made the sharp turn down the hill and under the wooden train truss. He was in the lead. Ryann slowed briefly to make the turn, then peddled hard again instead of coasting down the hill as usual. Skidding to a stop, tires burning two J-curved black streaks on the Thomas's driveway, Terell's lone voice rang out.

"Ha! I won!"

"Yeah, yeah," Ryann conceded with a quirky smile, "there's always a first time for everything."

The front door jerked open and Liddy raced out, slamming it behind her. "What's all the commotion?"

"Oh, it's Terell," Ryann answered matter-of-factly. "He needs to use your phone."

"What for?"

"To call the *Guinness Book of World Records* to report a first," Ryann droned, not cracking a smile.

Terell rolled his eyes. "Please, can't a guy just enjoy a win? I beat him here on our bikes."

"You guys are ridiculous," Liddy said, shaking her head. "Let's go around back to the deck. My mom is bringing out some lemonade."

Ryann took off ahead of Terell, hoping to regain his role of always being first. "You know what they say," Terell called out after him as Liddy and he strolled through the freshly mowed grass, "the first shall be last and the last shall be first."

Staring out over the water, Ryann went over his encounter with Gabriel in the castle chapel again. Recounting as many details as he could, Liddy listened intently and was concerned about one thing.

"Gabriel said the spirit will lead you and the ring *may* open the way?"

"Yeah," Ryann answered. "I was wondering about the change from '*will* open the way' to '*may* open the way' myself."

"*May, will*—what's the big difference?" Terell asked while slurping down the last bit of pale yellow liquid in his glass.

"Genius, it means that if the ring isn't helpful in getting back to Aeliana, then we'll have no way of knowing how to get there," Liddy responded half-jokingly, rolling her eyes.

"Back to square one," Ryann said, "with the exception of Gabriel allowing me to keep the ring, staff, and horn."

"Did he say anything about who the shield was for?" Liddy asked. "I mean, last time he said to find the *King's* sword."

"No. I just assumed it was for the King again. He did call it the shield of *faith*, though."

"Well. I just hope nothing happens while I'm gone," Liddy lamented. "As much as I love my grandparents and Rhode Island, it's no comparison to Aeliana."

"When do you get back?" Terell asked.

"The middle of August, the week before school starts."

Ryann looked at his watch. "Whoa. I'm supposed to meet Noah behind the church at eleven. I'd better get going, ten forty-five now."

"Me, too," Terell said. "Mom's got chores for me to do around the house."

Hopping up, Ryann tried to think of a way to say good-bye to Liddy. "Well, um, I guess this is it. We'll see you in a few months."

"Yeah, in a few months," Terell repeated awkwardly, looking down at the ground.

After all they had been through, Ryann felt like giving Liddy a hug goodbye, but his feet wouldn't move him any closer. Instead, he punched Terell in the arm, "Come on, let's go."

Scrambling off the deck to see who would be first back to their bikes, Terell yelled over his shoulder, "Have a great trip!"

Liddy yelled back, "Thanks! See ya soon!"

Ryann and Terell peddled up the embankment to Lake Shore Drive and stopped. Between breaths Terell asked, "So—what's the—next step?"

"If it's anything like last time, we'll stumble upon it when we're supposed to. In the meantime, I'm going to look up everything I can in my Bible software about shields."

"What about Drake?"

"Fortunately, it's summertime. I've never seen him much outside of school. I'm sure things will cool off between now and the end of August," Ryann reassured him.

"Let's hope so," Terell agreed. "Well, I'll see you around. Maybe we can go fishin' early tomorrow."

"Yeah, we'll see," Ryann answered as the pair split up with Terell heading back to his house and Ryann heading toward the church.

Lying fully stretched out on the bench behind the First Presbyterian Church, Noah's chest rose and fell rhythmically in the late morning shade. Ryann stared from ten feet away, recording mental notes of this simple man. Most of the townspeople considered him a harmless drifter. Some thought he was crazy; others viewed him as intelligent but with a dash of peculiarity thrown in. Ryann thought he was the perfect example of not judging a book by its cover. On the outside he had a roughly cut, salt-and-pepper colored beard, wrinkly weathered clothes, and shoes that looked like they might peel away at any moment. On the inside he possessed a genuine heart and a spirit to help people.

Ryann yelled between cupped hands. "Hey! Ol' man Noah, wake up!"

Noah didn't jump. That's the way he was. One eye opened to assess the situation, and then his mouth broke into a slight grin. "So, you're back, eh?"

"You betcha! And you're never gonna believe what happened."

Noah slowly pushed himself up, swinging his feet around to a sitting position. When satisfied he was comfortable, he patted the space next to himself. "Pull up a seat and tell me about it."

Ryann checked his watch. He had an hour until he needed to be home for lunch. Settling in next to the old man, Ryann quickly began relaying the account of his trials and tough times in Aeliana. Selfishly, he wanted to get to the encounter with Gabriel in the chapel so that he could hear Noah's comments.

"…and that's when he said I would need to seek out the shield of faith and that the ring *may* lead the way," Ryann concluded.

Noah had closed his eyes part-way through the story. Ryann knew he wasn't sleeping; it was Noah's way of thinking more deeply about a situation. Silent and still until Ryann was tempted to go over and shake him, he finally opened his eyes. Patiently waiting for his response, Ryann was drawn to the sparkling blueness of Noah's eyes. They were the one thing that made the elderly man seem so full of life.

"You handled yourself very well through the challenging situations in the cave," Noah commented.

"Thanks," Ryann shrugged uncomfortably. "But I don't understand why the Word would make it so difficult to reach the sword."

Noah smiled knowingly and slapped Ryann on the leg, "You should be happy when you encounter trials and tribulations!"

"Happy? Why would I be happy?" Ryann scrunched his face in a pained look.

"Because tribulation brings about perseverance; and perseverance, proven character."

"I guess I could be happier knowing that my persevering through tough times can actually result in something good in the future. I suppose it's part of having the right outlook on life."

"That's my boy. Now you're getting it."

Ryann decided to focus on something else. "Do you know anything about Lord Ekron?"

Ryann thought he saw Noah's eyes grow larger before he answered.

"I know that he is a great deceiver, who will even disguise himself as an angel of light to fool people. I believe he's what Gabriel was warning you about when you first came to speak to me, when he said your struggle is not against flesh and blood, but against the powers of this dark world and against the forces of evil in the heavenly realms."

"We never saw him again after defeating Drake and his army. Do you think he's gone for good?"

"No," Noah said, staring off dreamily, "the things which are seen are temporal, but the things which are not seen are eternal. I believe you will see Lord Ekron again. I'm sure he's not pleased with your success against him."

"Great, just great; sounds like more character building," Ryann laughed. "How 'bout the next task? I'm supposed to seek out the shield of faith."

Noah paused.

Ryann looked at his watch. "Whoa, it's almost noon, I have to get home for lunch." He hopped back on his bike and started to say goodbye, but Noah cut him off.

"One thing you should know, Ryann, is that faith is the assurance of things hoped for, the certainty of things not seen. Remember that this is what the ancients were commended for."

"Uhh, okay, I'll have to think about that. Let's talk again soon, Noah."

Noah's eyes sparkled. "I'm sure we will," he replied, smiling, as Ryann spun his bike around to leave.

Rising up in his seat, he started peddling away and heard Noah call out to him again. "Maybe those four buttons will light up on your next quest!"

"I didn't tell him about the buttons!" Ryann realized. He braked immediately and turned around. Noah had vanished.

With the wind blowing through his wispy blonde hair as he biked the short distance to his house, Ryann considered the unfathomable—was Noah actually Gabriel? He had read Bible stories of angels appearing on Earth as regular people, minus the wings. Mrs. Gigabund always reminded them of one of her favorite Bible verses during Sunday school: "Make sure that you show hospitality to strangers, because some people have entertained angels without knowing it." "The eyes," Ryann thought, "they both have those same sparkling blue eyes. I knew there was something about them."

Pepper's yappy bark, followed by his sister Alison yelling, broke Ryann away from his daydreaming. "Hey! You're just in time for lunch. Mom sent me out to look for you."

Ryann propped his bicycle up in the garage and trotted inside. Henry was already eating a few potato chips off his plate.

"Hey, son, did you get to say goodbye to Liddy?" Mr. Watters asked.

"Yes, Dad, she's gone until mid-August now."

"I'm thinking about us taking a trip this summer up to Annapolis. I'd like Henry to see what goes on during plebe summer at the Naval Academy. He's going into tenth grade now. You can never start planning for college too early. Right, Henry?"

"Sure, dad," Henry replied robotically. Ryann wasn't convinced Henry was so sure.

Typically, Ryann enjoyed mealtimes in the Watters's house. With all of the busy activities they were involved in, his parents made an effort to bring the family together. It also gave everyone an opportunity to share and hear about what was going on in each other's day. Today was different. Ryann felt as if he was lugging around a backpack full of bricks. He wasn't used to keeping things from his parents, and all of the supernatural happenings surrounding Aeliana and the sword were too much for him to bear alone. Sure, he had Terell and Liddy, and for that matter, even Noah...or was it Gabriel? They weren't a substitute for his parents. At first he was concerned that they would keep him from seeking the sword, then the longer he didn't say anything, the more awkward it felt to bring it up.

Ryann's brain was waging a little battle inside his head, "If you tell them, that's going to ruin everything. They'll never let you go back."

"Even when I don't agree with them, they do have my best interests at heart.

"They might ruin all the fun!

"If I'm truthful with them, I know I can trust them to do what's right."

"Dad?" Ryann heard himself interrupting his thoughts. "Uhh."

His parents both looked his way. "Do you and Mom have a few minutes after lunch to talk?" he quickly forced the words out of his mouth.

His father and mother's eyes met. "Sure son, we always have time to talk," his dad replied.

Alison stuck out her tongue and crossed her eyes when Ryann looked her way. After a few minutes of Henry talking about how he wanted to get a used car in the fall and Alison pestering Mom about going to the mall later in the afternoon, they finished and began cleaning up.

Retreating to his father's study, Ryann glanced around at the memorabilia on the walls, pictures of ships that his father had served on in the Navy, framed degrees from college and graduate schools, and awards for various accomplishments in business. His father always said that the most important things in life were your faith, family, and friends, and he kept pictures of the family around the desk he worked at as proof of that. Ryann focused in on several photos of the family over the years on vacations, as he plopped into one of the three leather chairs in the room. Squirming on the mushy leather seat, Ryann sat in silence, not sure how to begin.

"Well?" his father finally asked. "What did you want to talk about, Ryann?"

"It's kinda hard to start."

His father reached up and rubbed his smooth chin, looking at Ryann like he was peering into him. Then he spoke, "Do you want to tell us about Aeliana?"

"What...?" Ryann's jaw went slack. "How do you know about Aeliana?"

"Ryann," his mom answered in her caring voice, "we were visited by Gabriel the same night that you were. He told us what you had been chosen for and that we were not to bring it up with you until you came to us."

"So, so you've known the whole time?" He immediately thought about all of the opportunities that he had to discuss it with his parents.

"Yes, we have," she answered.

"You must think I'm terrible for not talking about it with you sooner," Ryann said, putting his head in his hands.

"Hey, hey. Hold your head up high, son," Mr. Watters said. "We're proud of you!"

"You are?"

"Sure, how many people do you think God chooses for a specific task? Not many, I'm sure," his dad continued. "Gabriel said you would face many challenges, and while I'm pretty sure we can't put it on your resume for college, we know now more than ever how special you are."

"Was it dangerous?" Mrs. Watters asked, with the concern of a mother.

"Oh! You have no idea, Mom. Dad, put your watch away," Ryann said grinning. "Have I got a story for you!"

ΑΩ

Afterword

PUT ON THE full armor of God so that you can take your stand against the devil's schemes. For our struggle is not against flesh and blood, but against the rulers, against the authorities, against the powers of this dark world and against the spiritual forces of evil in the heavenly realms. Therefore put on the full armor of God, so that when the day of evil comes, you may be able to stand your ground, and after you have done everything, to stand. Stand firm then, with the belt of truth buckled around your waist, with the breastplate of righteousness in place, and with your feet fitted with the readiness that comes from the gospel of peace. In addition to all this, take up the shield of faith, with which you can extinguish all the flaming arrows of the evil one. Take the helmet of salvation and the sword of the Spirit, which is the word of God.

—From a letter written by Saint Paul
to the church in Ephesus, 60 A.D.

To My Readers

TIME IS A precious thing. Thanks for using some of yours to read my book! *Ryann Watters and the Shield of Faith* is in the works. I feel as if I am back in the navy on the bridge of my ship, hours before the sun peaks over the horizon with a bitter cup of black coffee, as I carve out time to pursue this next adventure.

In the meantime... What can you do?

Take a few minutes to visit

www.RyannWatters.com

Growing up on adventure and fantasy novels, I enjoyed using my imagination to envision my favorite characters more fully. I loved seeing how artists captured the storylines and created colorful imagery. On the Ryann Watters Web site, you will see extensive artwork by the talented Corey Wolfe, who is responsible for the cover art, maps, and chapter images. In addition, we have real pictures of Mount Dora. See if what you pictured when Ryann was being chased through town matches up with the real thing!

HERE'S WHAT ELSE YOU WILL FIND ON THE WEB SITE:

- *Win autographed books from the author.*

- *Voice your opinion on possible future book covers.*

- *Hear Eric's vision behind his story.*

- *Be the first to receive exclusive updates.*

- *Get in on a drawing to choose the name of a key character in Book 2 of the trilogy.*

- *Q & A with the author and get real responses to your questions.*

- *Exciting new artwork by Corey Wolfe (plus visit his site at www.coreywolfe.com).*

- *Opportunities to set up autograph signings in your hometown.*

Thanks again,

Eric

It's your move!